The Elfdins and
the Gold Cross

Previously published with Resource Publications

Nonfiction

Storms Are Faith's Workout: Preparing Christians for Spiritual Ambush (2018).

Faith's Journey Confronts Obstacles: Instructing God's Soldiers to Overcome in His Armor (2019).

Satan's Strategy to Torment Through Physical Ambush: Educating God's Soldiers of Satan's Plot to Shatter Faith through Sickness and Disease (2019).

Spiritual Shipwreck on the Horizon: Exhorting Christians to Contend for the Faith and Comprehend the Deceitfulness of Sin (2019).

Satan Has No Authority Over God's Soldier: Illuminating Godlike Faith (2019).

God: The Holy Spirit: The Conquering Power Within (2019).

Signs of the Time: Warning: Lukewarm Christianity Accepts Deception (2020).

Flesh and Spirit Conflict: The Inner Battle of Choice (2020).

Supernatural Faith Disables: Quench the Fiery Darts (2020).

Seeds of Knowledge: Soil Determines the Seed's Harvest (2020).

Fiction

The Elfdins and the Gold Temple: An Oralee Chronicle (2018).

Charlie McGee and the Leprechaun: Life's Curious Twist of Events (2019).

The Shrines of Manitoba: Dark Secrets Shall Be Brought to Light (2019).

Guilty As Blood: One Can Make a Difference (2019).

Back From the Dead: Light Shines As the Noonday Sun (2020).

Nazis, Holocaust, and Self-Love: Unbridled Bigotry (2020).

Chateau de Paix: Nightmare Hiding In Paradise (2020).

The Elfdins and the Gold Cross

An Oralee Chronicle
Book 2

R. C. Jette

RESOURCE *Publications* · Eugene, Oregon

THE ELFDINS AND THE GOLD CROSS
An Oralee Chronicle: Book 2

Resource Publications
An Imprint of Wipf and Stock Publishers
199 W. 8th Ave., Suite 3
Eugene, OR 97401

www.wipfandstock.com

PAPERBACK ISBN: 978-1-6667-1258-2
HARDCOVER ISBN: 978-1-6667-1259-9
EBOOK ISBN: 978-1-6667-1260-5

All Scripture citations are taken from the KING JAMES VERSION (KJV):
KING JAMES VERSION, public domain.

08/03/21

This book is dedicated to my Lord Jesus Christ who makes the impossible achievable by faith.

To my husband (Paul) who has encouraged me to cross each Jordan I have encountered.

My daughter (Dawn) to whom words cannot convey my love and gratitude.

My son (PJ) his daughter (Kierra). My daughter (Christina) her sons (Andrew, Matthew, Joshua), her daughter (Sarah) with the Lord.

My mother (Rita Christina), my brothers (Frank and Raymond), my sister (Carol), my father-in-law (Albert), who are with the Lord, and other relatives awaiting the great reunion day.

Susanna and Mike for their help, and to all who have influenced my life throughout the years.

My special thanks is given to Wipf and Stock Publishers for publishing all my books under their Resource Publications.

I am grateful to Joe Delahanty, Jim Tedrick, Kara Barlow, Ian Creeger, and Stephanie Randels.

Special mention is given to Matthew Wimer, George Callihan, Shannon Carter, and Savanah N. Landerholm for their incredible help to get the books published.

He shall not be afraid of evil tidings: his heart is fixed, trusting in the Lord (Psalms 112:7).

Contents

Prologue

"WHAT IN TARNATION WAS that?" Prophet Andrew said, stumbling backwards as a ball of fire consumed the door of the building. Prophetess Deborah jumped out of her seat and stood next to Andrew. As they steadied themselves for what was about to come through the door, both were struck by bolts of lightning sending them on their backs to the floor, paralyzed, and powerless.

Next, they watched as three hideous black creatures walked through the doorway followed by a short figure dressed in black carrying an oak shillelagh. He stopped and gazed down at them. "It seems you Human Prophets are no match for me." He started to point his shillelagh at them and shook his head. "No." He snickered. "I'll just leave you both to watch me release Maddock from the invisible prison made by Great Prophet Godric." A glimmer of laughter came into his eyes. "This is more entertaining than I expected."

"Druxin, is that you?" Maddock said, behind his invisible prison wall.

"I became quite nettled trying to discover where you were." Druxin said, fingering his black beard with his right hand. "But I must admit it has been exhilarating to see these Humans so eager to tell me whatever I wanted to know." He sneered. "Of course, some probably wish they had complied sooner."

"Nobody is more powerful than Godric or Edith." Maddock said, bluntly. "How will you release me?"

"Just stand back against the far wall, close your eyes, and try to cover yourself."

"I'm back, and I've covered myself with my mattress."

Evil Druxin pointed his oak shillelagh in the direction of Maddock's voice and gave it a wave. Immediately there was a crackling fire. Behind it, a prison cell appeared.

A tall, gaunt Maddock dropped the mattress and stepped forward with wide eyes. "When I trained you in black power, I never dreamed you would be so powerful." He grabbed Druxin's right hand with both hands. "I'm so glad to see you." He brushed his long gray hair back with his hands. "I thought I was going to spend the rest of my life in that prison."

"It was incredible!" Evil said, laughing darkly. "Once I stepped into this world, I became unbelievably powerful. It must be that Oralee is a supernatural world and this being a natural world made my powers more enhanced." He chortled. "I'm unstoppable. Together we'll rule this world and prevent any Humans from getting back into Oralee."

Maddock's gaunt face screwed up. "Who are these Krogs? Where's Raven and Little Coal?"

Evil hung his head. "Little Coal was killed when I first started to make my move to take over Oralee. I am to blame, but I made them pay for it." He paused. "As for Raven, after we came through, he turned back into a normal cat and died."

"It's like his power became null and void in our world." Maddock said, his gray eyes squinting. "He reverted back to what he was before I brought him into Oralee." He paused. "I guess his old age couldn't be hidden in this natural world."

Druxin pointed to the three Krogs. "These are Carbon, Nightshade, and Soot; Raven and Little Coal's first litter. It seems all litters after these three became wild beasts who were killed in Oralee during the battle." He fingered his black beard with his right hand. "However, these three, like me, are more powerful here than in Oralee."

Maddock put up his right hand. "What's that noise?" He tilted his head to listen. "I believe the prophets are coming."

"I don't have time to deal with them at present," Evil said, swishing around them all with his shillelagh. "I want to meet your evil apprentices." He tapped his mouth with his right forefinger and whispered. "Don't speak, just follow me. They may sense something go by them, but they won't see what."

As the prophets and prophetesses ran towards Andrew and Deborah lying on the floor, Evil Druxin, Maddock, Carbon, Nightshade, and Soot quietly slipped out of sight.

Chapter 1

Déjà vu

"WHAT IN ORALEE IS happening?" Catrin said, pointing towards the Portal. "It's about to open."

"Warriors of the Sovereign God!" Griffin said, feeling his pulse race. "Stand guard."

Immediately, Master Drew, Mistress Meredith, and others joined Catrin and Griffin. As they stood ready, Old Chronicler, who appeared to be unconscious, fell through the Portal with his clothes shredded and bloodied.

Mistress Meredith and Catrin ran to him. "He's breathing." Meredith said, feeling his pulse. "Quickly! You men, carry him to the Healing Room." She said, hurrying ahead with Catrin following.

Patrick, Fletcher, Falconer, and Gwent carefully picked him up and followed Mistress Meredith and Catrin.

Rhonda ran behind. "This appears dreadful."

Owen shrugged his shoulders. "Precisely! He is in a disturbing condition."

David shook his head. "We've not seen anything like this since the Krogs."

"This is quite unnerving." Master Drew said, staying close to the others carrying Old Chronicler.

"It's like Déjà vu," Griffin said. "I remember being carried back on a stretcher after the Krog attacked me."

Owen threw up his hands. "I do not find any diversion in evoking those days."

"My sentiments entirely, my lad." Dylan said, touching Owen's right arm.

Kevyn shook his head. "Certainly, there's no more Krogs?"

Rhonda fidgeted with her left earlobe. "If you recollect, four of the horrendous creatures escaped with Evil Druxin through the Portal."

Owen grabbed his head both hands. "I had categorically forgotten about that."

As the men carefully placed Old on the table. "Mistress Meredith." Catrin said. "I believe this evil is more powerful than the Krog attacks we had here. There's a vile sense coming through."

"I sense it is more vile than we've ever encountered." Mistress Meredith said, nodding her head. "Let's lay our hands on Old and invoke the Sovereign God's healing power."

As she and Catrin laid hands on Old, Meredith nodded her head towards Catrin. "Please pray. I'm still trying to get used to the Sovereign God's supernatural power and not reach for my herbal remedies."

"Sovereign God." Catrin said. "You are Jehovah Rapha, *the Lord that healeth*, and you promise in your word *they shall lay hands on the sick, and they shall recover.* In your name, Old be healed!"

As Griffin listened to Meredith and Catrin, he scratched the back of his head with his right hand. "I don't mean to frighten anyone, but Catrin and my Ma are correct. I sense an incredible evil on the other side of the Portal."

"We'll need to watch the Portal day and night." Master Drew said, rubbing his chin with his right hand. "It's like when we had to keep watch at the entrance to the Gold Mountain."

Rhonda did a two-step. "However, we are not merely physical warriors anymore. We are supernatural warriors of the Sovereign God." She shot her left fist into the air. "We must never neglect that."

"Amen! All of us have supernatural capabilities," Dylan said. "Some are more powerful than others, but together we are most formidable."

"We are to stand in the power of his cross clothed in his full armor." Patrick said, folding his arms.

Suddenly David pointed towards the Portal. "It's opening! Get ready!"

All but Mistress Meredith and Catrin ran towards the Portal.

Gwent gave out a heavy sigh. "Time to show how formidable we are."

Everyone stood silent as Master Godric Halig came running through, pausing to catch his breath. "Thank the Sovereign God you're all here. It's an incredible evil out there." He sat to gain his composure. "Edith and I are powerless against Evil Druxin. We have avoided him while trying to get as many to the place of refuge as we could."

"What do you mean you're powerless against him?" Griffin said, his eyebrows squishing together." You and Edith are the two most powerful Humans."

Godric's voice lowered. "Yes, we are. However, when we were told Evil Druxin released Maddock from our prison, we knew he used a power beyond ours. That's why we've steered clear of him." He sighed, heavily. "It was vital to find as many as possible to hide. Sir Archibald was trying to get in here to let you know what has happened in our world, when he was attacked by one of Druxin's Krogs." His face screwed up. "His nephew Sir Richard Oswald and I were close behind when it came out of nowhere. I sent a ball of fire that sent it fleeing." He shrugged his shoulders. "When I turned to help Archibald, he was falling through the Portal." He gestured with his right hand. "Sir Richard stayed behind in a cloak of invisibility to keep watch." He rubbed his chin with his right hand. "We believed Sir Reginald was finished." He let out a huge breath. "That's why I had to get through to inform you what's happening in our world."

Owen gestured with both hands. "Great Jehoshaphat! It was a Krog incident."

As they were all gazing at Owen, Sir Archibald, known as Old Chronicler, sat next to Godric. "Lordy me! It looks like these Elfdins have powers beyond yours." He laughed. "I thought I was about to be part of history."

Godric's eyes bulged. "Bless the Sovereign God! You're alive." He gave Old a hug with tears streaming down his cheeks.

"This is a supernatural world after all." Owen said, combing his ash blond hair back with the fingers of his left hand.

Godric grabbed his head with both hands. "That's why Evil Druxin has more power. He entered into a natural world from a supernatural world. He's a supernatural being in a world inhabited with natural beings." He bit his bottom lip. "I should have realized that." He threw up his hands. "But all we thought of, when we entered our world fifteen days ago to find what looked like a war zone, was to get our families to a place of refuge before Druxin and Maddock realized who was who." He paused. "From what we were told, Druxin had his attention focused on finding Maddock and meeting his evil apprentices." He gestured with his right hand. "That's why we were able to get all our families to the place of refuge in the old forest without anyone knowing what we were doing." He sighed, heavily. "Druxin's cruelty knew no boundary while hunting for Maddock."

Master Drew rubbed his chin with his right hand. "I keep forgetting about the time difference. We've gone through another year here, and you've only been there fifteen days."

Old sat back and shook his head. "Evil Druxin had been there fifteen days before we returned, and our world looked as though we had been at war for years." He gestured with his right hand. "He wreaked destruction and devastation in such a short time trying to locate Maddock."

Godric shook his head and blinked his eyes. "Wait a minute! What kind of power do you have to heal Old like that?" He threw up both hands. "I was certain the Krog killed him."

"After we believed in the power of the Sovereign God's cross, we all received our supernatural powers." Griffin said.

Dylan gestured towards Mistress Meredith and Catrin. "Through the laying on of hands, the Great Prophetesses have phenomenal healing ability, next is the Great Prophets, then the Spiritual Mentors." He shrugged his shoulders. "As a matter of fact, all Elfdins over thirteen have healing power to some degree."

Godric's eyebrows squished together. "If you have that power here, how much greater would it be in our world?" He paused. "I mean, Druxin has paralyzed two of our students who were guarding Maddock's prison." His eyes filled with tears. "Prophet Andrew and Prophetess Deborah were the two most promising in the Prophet's School, and now they can't speak or move." He paused. "We're feeding them liquid through a thin tube that we slip down their throat."

Catrin punched the air with her fist. "We can't stay in Oralee while evil is trying to overtake their world." She clenched her teeth. "How can we remain living our daily lives as if nothing is happening, when such wickedness is about to destroy their world?" She paused. "I mean, can't we go through the Portal and help them?"

Winifred put her left hand on Catrin's right shoulder. "Catrin, my lass, I agree with you. However, how would we get back without a gold cross?"

Old held up his gold cross. "One of you could use mine." "Lordy me!" He said, clasping his hands together. "At my age, I'm no help against supernatural evil."

Godric looked at his gold cross. "I know I'm no match against Druxin, but I am against Maddock and his evil apprentices." He hung his head. "My world is in chaos, and they all look to me for guidance. I believe I must be in my world."

Catrin's eyebrows scrunched together. "I don't really understand what I'm hearing, but I believe the Sovereign God is instructing me to go back with you. He's telling me to *trust in the Lord with all thine heart; and lean not unto thine own understanding. In all thy ways acknowledge him, and he shall direct thy paths.*"

Griffin grabbed her right hand with both his hands. "I'm not letting you go through that Portal without me." He paused. "Besides the Sovereign God says, *he shall not be afraid of evil tidings:*

his heart is fixed, trusting in the Lord. I believe we're being told evil tidings await us in the Human World, but we're not to be afraid."

Catrin punched the air with her right fist. "We trust in our Sovereign God."

"I don't grasp what's transpiring, but I'm accompanying you." Rhonda said, matter-of-factly.

"Pause one confounded minute!" Owen said. "I will be incorporated in this Crusade."

Dylan gestured with both hands. "I, indubitably, am included."

David paced back and forth. "I'm going with you all. However, there's only one gold cross, how will all of us get back in?"

Meghan twisted her hands. "Well, I'm not staying here if David's going there."

Patrick pointed towards the Portal. "I'm not remaining behind while my bairns are going through that Portal. I led the last Crusade. If that's what has to be done, I'll do so again."

Winifred sat down and looked at everyone. "I will not stay back this time. I intend to fight alongside my family."

Master Drew rubbed his chin with his right hand. "The Sovereign God wanted me on the last Crusade, and it's no different this time."

"I believe I'm with Winifred." Mistress Meredith said. "We stayed behind last time, but the Crusaders traveling in Oralee was different than entering an unknown world. I may be more needed there than here."

"Count me and Kevyn in." Gwent said.

"Wait a minute!" Gwendolyn said. "If my husband and lad are going, so am I."

Archer grabbed his head with both hands. "All I know is this feels like déjà vu as Griffin said. I'm definitely coming."

"Me too." Falconer said. "I don't believe my falcons will be any use in an unknown world for messaging. However, I will not be left out of this Crusade."

Fletcher shrugged his shoulders. "I was part of the last Crusade, and I intend to be part of this one."

Vanora's voice trembled. "Can we hide little Rhett with your families in the place of refuge? I'm not about to stay behind with my whole family going through the Portal."

Prophet Godric threw up both hands. "Of course. However, all you that leave, will not be able to get back."

Catrin twirled her raven black hair around her right finger. "I believe the Sovereign God is telling us to step out on the water like Peter."

Griffin scratched the back of his head with his right hand. "He's telling me, *I will instruct thee and teach thee in the way which thou shalt go: I will guide thee with mine eye.* He paused. "I believe he's confirming that we can't lean to our own understanding, for he'll guide us in the way to go."

Patrick folded his arms. "I think they're both right."

Prophet Godric sighed, heavily. "I don't know if you're all comprehending what this means. Do you realize you'll never be able to get back into Oralee?"

Meghan's eyes widened. "That means we'll be separated for life."

Catrin threw up her arms. "Then why don't we all leave. All the ancestrals and parents who need to stay with their bairns can be protected in your place of refuge. Since all of us will have supernatural powers in the Human World, it may take all of us to overcome Druxin's evil."

Kevyn's eyebrows squished together. "Shouldn't we have some of the Pundles come with us to protect the place of refuge?" He shrugged his shoulders. "After all they were more powerful than the Krogs here. Wouldn't they be more powerful than the Krogs there?"

Owen kicked the ground with his left foot. "Absolutely! That's an astounding idea." He patted Kevyn on the back with his left hand. "Exceptional!"

"If we're all leaving, why would any of the Pundles remain here?" Meghan said, twisting her hands.

Mistress Meredith closed her eyes and rubbed her forehead with her right hand. "I believe the Pundles would rather be with us. We've become so attached to them and they to us." She gestured with her right hand. "It only seems right for us to all leave together."

Rhonda fidgeted with her left ear lobe. "But that will abandon Old. He will be entirely isolated. Who will monitor him?" Her face flushed. "I know the Sovereign God *will never leave nor forsake him.*" Her face screwed up. "Who will nourish him?"

Old sat down and folded his arms. "Lordy me! Let me tell you young spiritual mentor about my earlier days. Before I became a knight, I used to work in the kitchen of a lord. I'm a skilled cook." His eyes took on a strange look. "I feel strongly I must stay here. However, I do understand about the time difference." He scratched the back of head with his right hand. "I believe the Sovereign God is prompting me not to concern myself about it. You see, when we return through the Portal, we have only aged fifteen days for each year here." He patted Rhonda's left hand with his right hand. "I'm in the Sovereign God's hands. Can't be any better than that."

Godric touched Old's arm. "Sir Archibald, you could stay in the place of refuge with the others." He said, his face screwing up. "If you desire, you could stay with me and the others that come to Oralee." He paused, "But that is much farther away than the place of refuge."

Old shook his head. "The Sovereign God wants me to stay here. I must obey. Remember, *to obey is better than sacrifice.*"

Godric chuckled. "It should have been me saying that." He paused. "Sir Archibald is right. We must obey the Sovereign God even when we don't understand."

Patrick rubbed his temple with his right hand. "Well, let's get through to the Human World as soon as possible before Druxin senses what we're doing."

Griffin bowed his head. "Sovereign God, please let the ancestrals, parents with bairns get safely to the place of refuge. Help the members of the Crusade to safely reach Mistress Edith and the others."

"Amen!" They all said in unison.

Chapter 2

The Exodus

PROPHET GODRIC WENT BACK through the Portal to make sure there were no more Krogs waiting and to check on Sir Richard. He made an invisible shield around to protect the Elfdins exit and informed Sir Richard of what was to transpire. "The Elfdins are leaving their world to help us battle Evil Druxin and the evil endeavoring to destroy our world." His voice shook. "It means they're willingly leaving Oralee without the means to return."

"Excuse me." Sir Richard said, his voice revealing stress. "How is my uncle?"

"Oh my!" Godric said, clutching his hands together. "He's completely healed." He patted Richard on the back. "Oralee is a supernatural world, and the Elfdins possess incredible supernatural powers from the Sovereign God I wasn't even aware of."

"No wonder Evil Druxin is so powerful in our world."

"Exactly!" Godric said. "That's why the Elfdins are leaving Oralee to help us battle the supernatural evil of Druxin." His face screwed up. "They know the only way to combat evil is for all Sovereign God warriors to unite and take on the malevolence in his full armor." He pointed towards the Portal. "It may take a couple of days for them to start exiting, but we'll stand guard until they do."

It was decided that Master Drew and Mistress Meredith would go through first in case Master Godric was not able to secure the exit.

All would go through the Portal by twos with two Pundles behind them. Following High Prophet Drew and High Prophetess Meredith would be Griffin and Catrin, Owen and Rhonda, Dylan and Kevyn, Patrick and Winifred, David and Meghan, Gwent and Gwendolyn, Falconer Hopper and Heidi, Fletcher Prichard and Ariana.

All others were to wait until Heidi, using Old's gold cross, came back through to let them know everything was set to start the Exodus into the Human World. Following Heidi through would be Archer and Vanora carrying young Rhett, then all warriors. Next would be all those thirteen and older. Then parents with young bairns. All the ancestrals were to come through last.

As each Elfdin stepped up to the Portal, Sir Archibald known as Old Chronicler said, "Godspeed!" After the last two went through, he sat down and gazed at the Puns who were to remain to keep him company. They were two of the oldest that had guarded his castle while he was gone. "Well, Pearl and Pemberton, it's you and me." He threw his head back and let out a peal of laughter. "The Sovereign God knew how bonded we are and used this time for us to have fellowship without distractions." He paused. "Lordy me!" He said, scratching the back of his head with his right hand. "It appears we are to stay in the Temple and not at our castle." He stood up. "Well, let's get all we'll need from the castle and bring everything into the Healing Room."

He gathered what was essential for the time being and packed them on the backs of Pearl and Pemberton. Other provisions were packed in bags, if needed, the Puns would fetch them from the castle. Once in the Gold Temple, he stored everything in the Healing Room. "Lordy me! I do feel such an excitement about this whole situation." He clasped his hands together. "My pets, I have such a sense of expectation."

As soon as Drew and Meredith stepped into the Human World, they were met with an evil that chained them in invisible bonds. "I can't move!" Drew said.

Meredith collapsed as her knees gave out. "I'm in chains, but I can't see them." She paused. "How can we help the others?"

"This shroud of darkness has me unable to see you or myself." Drew said, shakingly. "I feel one of the Pundles trying to release me. Whatever evil this is, it has no effect upon them."

"Oh no! I hear the Portal. We can't warn them." Meredith said.

Griffin and Catrin came through and immediately were chained in invisible bonds. "Catrin! Griffin! We're in some unseen chains." Meredith said. "This darkness is like a shroud hiding any light."

Catrin stood with shoulders back, chest out, and chin high. "*He brought them out of darkness and the shadow of death and brake their bands in sunder.* Sovereign God, I stand in your armor and command the darkness and chains to be shattered." Immediately, the light shone through, the chains broke, and fell to the ground.

Master Drew helped Meredith up. "This was meant to stop Elfdins from coming through the Portal, that's why it was no impediment for Master Godric."

Griffin nodded his head. "Yes, I see Godric and Sir Richard standing off to the left." He pointed towards the Portal. "Yet, there are no chains near the Pundles."

Master Drew nodded his head. "Yes. One was trying to release me during the darkness."

"Apparently, the Krog is no longer here." Griffin said. "Druxin must have believed his evil shroud and chains would stop any Elfdins from entering the Human World."

"This evil is nothing like we experienced all the time Druxin was in Oralee." Catrin said, her eyebrows scrunching together. "It appears his supernatural powers are more enhanced in this natural world."

Griffin nodded his head. "*Thy word is a lamp unto my feet, and a light unto my path.* Praise the Sovereign God for his word."

Meredith hugged Catrin. "I believe I really must get my mind on the power of his word and not the natural means I spent my life relying upon."

Drew hung his head. "It seems I, too, am guilty of that."

"Without the word, we have no power in the natural." Catrin said.

"In the natural, we used bows and arrows." Griffin said, scratching the back of his head with his right hand. "Now we battle in the supernatural with his two-edged sword."

"We need to be watchful!" Meredith said. "Let's continue to make a wall for the others to come through, in case there's something else set up." She gestured towards the Portal. "If it affected Drew and me, it could be worse for others without our power or ability."

"I believe the Sovereign God's word has dispelled the evil." Catrin said, gesturing with both hands. "But there could be a backup plan, so we better stand ready."

They stood still as Owen and Rhonda came through.

Rhonda's eyes bulged. "Great Jehoshaphat! What are those chains?"

Owen shook his head. "Ghastly!"

Griffin gestured with his right hand. "We'll explain after. At present, we must guard the Portal for the others to come out. Just continue our wall."

After the last of the Elfdins were out, Prophet Godric addressed Drew and Meredith. "I heard the Portal open, heard you both, but saw nothing." He gestured towards Catrin. "Once she prayed to the Sovereign God, everything became normal." His face screwed up. "It's imperative for some of you to be with us who have been in Oralee. After what I just witnessed, we need to join our heads together to combat this evil." He rubbed his chin with his right hand. "Whatever powers Edith and I have here seem to be useless against Druxin. It will take your supernatural power to overcome him."

Dylan nodded his head. "I was pondering that all who accompanied the last Crusade along with their families are significantly formidable, and should be in on all strategies formulated."

Patrick ran his fingers along the scar from his right temple to his chin. "That's what I thought." He pointed to all the warriors.

"These others, who are not going to the place of refuge will have to be put in another place of safety until we know what's what."

"That looks like a great place for everyone to make a camp." Mistress Meredith said, pointing to a nearby mountain. "I know you're concerned about your power against Druxin, but I do believe you can cause the camp to become invisible." She said, motioning towards Godric.

"Certainly! I've done so at the place of refuge." Godric said. "Let me just make an invisible wall around all the ancestrals, bairns, and parents who have to stay with them." He paused. "We should have time, from what I've heard, Druxin and Maddock are busy with Maddock's evil apprentices." He chuckled. "Besides, it seemed Druxin thought he had the Portal fixed to stop any Elfdins from coming through."

"Patrick rubbed his right temple with his right hand. "Do you have any idea what Druxin and Maddock are planning?"

"None." He pointed to the bairns, parents, and ancestrals. "Let's get them protected." He immediately put an invisible wall around the parameter outside the Portal. "Now," he said, sighing, "let's get the rest of you up that mountain."

As they were walking up the path towards the mountain, Catrin questioned Godric. "If the Humans in the place of refuge have never seen or heard about Oralee and the Elfdins, how will you explain who we are?"

Rhonda fidgeted with her left earlobe. "My conception, precisely."

Godric rubbed his forehead with his right hand. "I hadn't thought about that." His face screwed up. "I don't know what to tell them."

Catrin gestured with both hands. "All I know is I'm to accompany you." She paused. "First, we need to get all these situated, and we'll see what the Sovereign God wants us to tell those who have never heard of Oralee." She twirled her raven black hair around her right forefinger. "It will be quite shocking for them to see little people dressed in forest green attire."

Griffin nodded his head. "Yes! It will be quite a sight." He scratched the back of his head with his right hand. "At present, we need to move forward. We'll face that obstacle when it happens."

David clasped his hands together. "We need to move quickly."

"I deduce we will maintain certain Pundles in the camp." Dylan said. "They will assist to transport things."

"Thank the Sovereign God!" Griffin said, rubbing his hands together while observing the area. "This will be sufficient to hide the warbands."

"There are numerous huge caves in the mountain that will be great housing." Patrick said, running his fingers along the scar from his right temple to his chin.

"Okay!" Master Drew said. "Let's get everyone housed according to families." He gestured towards Patrick. "Then Prince Patrick will divide everyone in warbands."

After Patrick divided them up in warbands, he motioned for them to be quiet. "I believe we need to be ready to take on anything." He rubbed his right temple with his right hand. "I don't know how long the members of the Crusade will be away or how long before we'll be calling certain warbands to mobilize. However, I've asked my cousin, Dewey Ryn, to be in control of the camp." Patrick paused. "He'll be appointing certain warriors of the Sovereign God to help him lead." He placed his right hand on Dewey's left shoulder. "He would've been part of the first Crusade had he not been recovering from a Krog attack." He paused. "This is one powerful soldier, and he'll lead the first warband out of here when needed."

Sir Richard interrupted. "Should I stay at the Portal and not follow you to the place of refuge? After all, my uncle is still in Oralee."

Griffin shook his head. "I believe you are to stay with us. Your uncle is quite safe."

Herald Roth gestured with his left hand. "I keep feeling someone should be at the Portal." He scratched the back of his head with his left hand. "I don't know why, but I would like to volunteer for it."

"I believe he's correct." Griffin said.

Catrin nodded her head. "It doesn't make sense since we're all here, but I believe he needs to be there."

Herald gazed at Master Godric. "Could you make an invisible wall around me with an opening allowing me to get out if I have to?"

"Of course. I'll leave an opening in the back towards the woods. You can just put branches and leaves to cover it."

Herald nodded his head. "I'll take what I'll need and my Pundle to help me."

Godric sighed, heavily. "I feel strongly for us to get the others into the place of refuge."

Griffin made a tent with his fingers and tapped his lips with his forefingers. "I firmly sense all the warriors of the First Crusade and families should accompany you to the place of refuge. From there, we can follow you to Mistress Edith, High Prince Ordway, High Princess Ardith Heather, and the rest."

Godric finished securing the mountain camp, and sighed, heavily. "Okay. Let's get down to the others and get them to the place of refuge quickly." He paused. "I just wish I could shake this feeling of foreboding. I sense something, but I can't get a grasp on it."

"I know, it's like when we had to join the Crusade." Meghan said, twisting her hands.

Catrin's eyebrows scrunched together. "I don't want to affright anyone, but I feel we must get there quickly." She gestured with both hands. "There's something quite troubling at the place of refuge."

Griffin scratched the back of his head with his right hand. "I've been getting the same vibes." He gestured with his right hand. "I feel they're safe, but something is wrong."

Patrick rubbed his right temple with his right hand. "Let's be calm." He paused. "I've not known Catrin or Griffin to be wrong about things. However, we must move quickly."

"Let's start down and move swiftly." Mistress Meredith said, nodding her head.

While they were walking, Owen gestured with both hands. "I covet methods of journeying more swiftly."

Godric's face screwed up. "We have horses, but I don't believe any of you know how to ride."

"Horses!" Rhonda said.

"What's that?" David said, his eyebrows squishing together.

"They're animals who are our means of transportation." Godric said. "We never brought any into Oralee after we saw how huge the dogs became when entering."

"Okay." Gwent said. "What are dogs?"

"They're known as Pundles in Oralee. But here, they're much smaller." He chuckled. "Horses are much larger than the Pundles in our world. We couldn't imagine how huge they would be in Oralee." He paused. "There are many at the place of refuge. Perhaps, we can see if there are any small enough for the warriors of the Crusade to ride."

"Let's move quickly towards the others." Griffin said. "The faster we get them to safety, the swifter we can get on with the business of stopping Evil Druxin."

"Yes." Catrin said, her eyebrows scrunching together. "Also, we need to find out what is going on at the refuge."

"In the meantime, we have to make sure all is well with bairns and ancestrals." Winifred said, biting her bottom lip.

"I'll run ahead and make sure all is safe." Falconer said.

"Let me join you." Fletcher said, running to keep up.

They ran ahead and stood near where the invisible wall should be and waited for everyone to get there. "I believe this is the place where the ancestrals, bairns, and parents are." Falconer said, pointing to his left.

Godric smiled. "That's correct." He quickly lowered the wall, set up Herald Roth in a secure place near the forest, and left an opening for him to put branches to hide it. Finishing, he clutched his hands together. "We really must move swiftly to the place of refuge."

"I detect the identical urgency." Rhonda said, fidgeting with her left earlobe.

"Incredible!" Owen said. "That is my precise assessment."

As they hurried, Vanora touched her husband's left arm with her right hand. "Archer, I truly believed I was to accompany the Crusade, but I now sense the Sovereign God wants me to stay at the place of refuge with young Rhett." She paused. "I'm quite addled."

Archer nodded his head. "While I've been walking and carrying him, I sensed the same thing. I, too, am muddled."

Vanora rubbed her arms with both hands. "All I know is I must stay with our bairn."

Godric interrupted them, pointing to his right. "Just ahead at that old forest is the place of refuge. The invisible cloak hides all Humans and livestock. Otherwise, the forest appears normal." He paused. "I'll have to lead and make an opening for everyone to follow me in."

Before he could do as he said, Catrin kept walking with Griffin, David, Meghan, Rhonda, and Owen right through the wall and disappeared from sight. As they appeared inside the cloak, Susanna, the niece of Princess Ardith Heather, stood with eyes wide-opened. "Who in tarnation are you little people? Why are you dressed in forest green? Where did you come from? How did you get through the invisible cloak created by Master Godric?"

David rubbed the back of neck with his right hand. "Master Godric is behind us. We've come to help."

As Godric joined them, he stood rubbing his chin with his right hand. "Baffling!" He said. "I believe there's more unknown power being discovered."

"Master Godric!" Susanna said, running to him. "Something terrible is going on."

"What do you mean?" Godric said, his face screwing up.

"Many have come down with a sickness." She gestured with both hands. "We don't know what to do." She caught her breath. "Prophetess Christina is the best herbalist around, but she has been unsuccessful." Her eyes filled with tears. "Some are near death."

"Mistress Meredith!" Catrin said, hurrying to Meredith. "Many of the Humans have an unknown sickness. We've got to get to them quickly. Some are near death."

"Quickly!" Griffin said, gesturing with both hands. "Take us to the sick."

"Yes. Follow me. We have them all in the Great Hall in the castle." Susanna threw up both hands. "It was the only place large enough to keep an eye on everyone. However, the ones tending them are getting sick."

Catrin, Mistress Meredith, and others quickly followed Susanna and Griffin. "Great Jehoshaphat!" Owen said, observing all the sick.

"They do appear indisposed." Rhonda said, her face screwing up.

"Well." Dylan said, stroking his chin with fingers of his left hand. "I ascertain those more afflicted will be tended to by Catrin and Mistress Meredith on down according to our positions."

Catrin stood still, bowed her head, and prayed. "Sovereign God, we need help. I sense an evil in here. There's someone in here who is an apprentice of the evil prophet, Maddock." She gazed at the Humans. "He has brought in this sickness."

She no sooner finished when Michael, cousin to Susanna, fell to the ground crying. "I am the one to blame." He held up a vial. "I was told that anytime we had harmful water, I was to put in this, and it would be purified." He sniffled. "Our water in the well seemed to be putrid." He gazed at Catrin. "I was following him, but I began to feel something wrong." His chin trembled. "Believe me I had no idea any evil was in the vial until you prayed." He gestured towards the sick. "These are my family and friends." He wiped his eyes with his right hand. "Please! Can you help them?"

Griffin scratched the back of head with his right hand. "We must destroy the evil in the vial." He took the vial from Michael and with a ball of fire destroyed it."

Susanna, Michael, and other Humans jumped back with eyes bulged. Michael gazed at Master Godric. "What kind of power do these little people have to do that?"

Owen kicked the ground with his left foot. "Our power is supernatural from the Sovereign God."

"Okay!" Mistress Meredith said. "It's time to get busy with our responsibility to heal these Humans." She gestured towards Susanna. "You know who are the sickest. Catrin and I will take care of them."

Dylan nodded his head. "Yes, then navigate us to individuals who are less ill, etc."

Rhonda fidgeted with her left earlobe. "We all comprehend our degree of competence. You just divulge the severest on down, we will proceed accordingly."

Michael's voice trembled. "Please, take care of my mother. She is about the sickest."

Catrin touched his right arm. "Lead me to her."

Griffin observed the Humans and sensed the Sovereign God direct him to what would heal them all quickly. "Excuse me!" He said to Prophetess Christina. "Do you have any type of poison?"

Christina's face screwed up. "Poison?"

Griffin nodded his head. "The Sovereign God is saying to treat poison with poison."

Christina's eyes widened. "Okay." She said, her voice barely audible. "I have mandrake, hemlock, belladonna."

"Mandrake!" He said. "I believe we have to give everyone the mandrake." He scratched the back of his head with his right hand. "I have no idea what it is or how it's administered, so you will have to explain it to us."

Owen gestured with both hands. "Hasten! We must proceed immediately."

Prophetess Christina motioned towards Michael. "Help me get it."

Christina quickly returned with Michael following. "Here it is." She said. "I have enough to administer to all the sick."

Griffin rubbed his hands together. "Okay, tell us what to do. We must all work swiftly."

"Everyone is to receive one spoonful." Christina handed a vial and a spoon to everyone. "This is most strange." Her eyebrows squished together. "I've used it for severe pain. However, I never thought to use it for this."

Rhonda felt an adrenaline rush. "My heart is hammering. I sense such exhilaration."

Catrin administered the first spoonful to Golda, Michael's mother. "Be healed in the name of the Sovereign God."

Golda's eyes opened and she sat up with Michael giving her a big hug. "Mother! You're healed."

David's hands trembled as he gave his first dose. "I pray the Sovereign God touches this old man."

He no sooner administered the dose, when the man's eyes opened, and he sat up. "Who in tarnation are you?"

"I am Prince David of the Elfdins." David said, his mouth gaping open.

Before the old man could respond, all the Humans were sitting up one after the other. Same as the old man, all asked the same question of their Elfdin healers.

Griffin jumped up. "We must get all the water in here back in the well. If we don't neutralize the water, all will be sick again." He gazed at Christina. "Do you have more of this mandrake?"

"I have plenty of the plants."

Griffin scratched the back of head with his right hand. "I have no idea what kind of plant it is."

"I'll get one." Michael said, rushing to get one.

As soon as Michael retrieved a mandrake, he handed it to Griffin. "The roots are rather strange looking plants resembling Humans."

"Wow! What odd plants." Griffin said, nodding his head. "I don't believe we have anything like this where we're from." He paused. "We need to chop up one plant, throw the pieces in the well, and it should immediately neutralize the poison."

"I don't know what to say." Michael said, hugging Griffin. "You saved my mother and all the rest." His eyes filled with tears. "How do young people get caught up into thinking evil power is good? I was supposed to be in the church, but I thought it was too boring." He rubbed his chin with his right hand. "After seeing what the Sovereign God does through all of you. I believe I want to learn healing."

Patrick ran his fingers along the scar from his right temple to his chin. "Warriors, I believe we need to get on with our Crusade. Druxin and Maddock are conjuring up evil, and we must be prepared to combat it."

"I agree." Godric said, clutching his hands together. "We really must meet up with the others."

Vanora gave Archer a hug. "The Sovereign God will protect you." Then she gestured towards Michael. "I believe I can be of help to you with healing herbs." She giggled. "After all my mother is the Great Prophetess Meredith of the Elfdins. Before we had the supernatural power from the Sovereign God, we were proficient in healing herbs."

"Where do you Elfdins come from?" Golda said, her eyebrows squishing together. "We've never heard of an Elfdin before today."

"We come from a faraway land." Vanora said, her face screwing up. "In time you'll know more."

Godric gave out a heavy sigh. "However, in the meantime, we have to be prepared to combat the evil trying to overtake our land."

The Elfdins were to ride the children's horses fitted with youth saddles. Being supernatural beings, they seemed to take to riding as though they had done it their whole life.

"I really do enjoy riding." Winifred said, her face beaming. "It's quite exciting."

"Remarkable!" Owen said, gesturing with his left hand. "Quite fascinating."

"Superlative!" Rhonda said, shooting her left fist up in the air. "This is most enthralling."

David rubbed the back of head with his right hand. "I wish we had horses in Oralee."

"Me too." Meghan said. "This is agreeable."

After travelling sometime, Godric motioned with his right hand. "I need everyone to listen. After this clearing is another forest. It's tricky, so everyone must stay close behind each other. Inside the forest are underground caverns with tunnels leading to a huge cavern that I'm sure no one besides my family knows about. It was used as a secret shelter during the last war." He paused. "My grandfather left the castle and the forest with the underground cavern to me." He rubbed his chin with his right hand. "He discovered the cave quite accidently. Apparently, he was hunting, and his hound ran through a waterfall. At first, he thought his hound was hurt and ran after him. Next thing he knew, he was inside a cavern. He pointed to his right. "The opening into the forest is about five furlongs ahead."

"What's a hound?" Meghan said.

"It's a breed of dog for hunting." Godric said, smiling. "Not the same breed as the Pundles."

Catrin's eyebrows scrunched together. "I sense evil. It's just ahead." She paused. "Is there a way around?"

"No!" Godric said. "We have to enter the forest from this direction in order to get to the underground cavern." He gestured towards his right. "If we come in the other way, we'll have to climb down the mountain leading to the waterfall. The horses won't be able to do it, and it's quite dangerous even for us."

Mistress Meredith leaned forward on her horse. "Catrin's right, there's something vile ahead."

Griffin glanced around, cautiously. "Master Godric! We really must get us lined up in order of our ability." He paused. "I mean no offense, but you and Sir Richard must get in the rear. The evil ahead is not of this world." His face screwed up. "I sense something more malevolent than we've faced so far."

Chapter 3

Evil Has No Conscience

EVIL DRUXIN GAZED AT Raven's body. "I know my pet. I'll not quit until I revenge your death." He was interrupted as Maddock came into the room. "Well, Maddock, have you rallied all your apprentices?"

Maddock brushed his long gray hair back with his hands. "I believe we have quite a formidable group of evil apprentices who are eager to learn more from you." He sneered. "It still amazes me how powerful you are in my world."

Druxin fingered his beard, leaned back in his chair, and folded his arms. "When I was forced to leave Oralee, I was quite agitated." He motioned with his right hand toward his pipe on a table across the room that was immediately in his hand. "This time, I'll not only take over this world, but I'll once and for all destroy the Sovereign God." He snarled. "I'll prevent any Humans from entering Oralee." He lit his pipe with his right forefinger. "As for the Elfdins, they won't come here."

"Why wouldn't they come here?" Maddock said, his gray eyes squinting.

"They don't have a gold cross to get back." He snickered. "Besides, I left a little present for any Elfdin who may decide to leave."

Maddock threw up his arms. "I guess I thought it was only Humans who needed a gold cross to get in." He smirked. "That will make things easier to control this world."

"Have you located anyone who can tell us about Master Godric, Mistress Edith, Prince Ordway, Princess Ardith Heather, and the others?"

"As a matter of fact, a few of my choice pupils have four squires who work for Prince Ordway and Princess Ardith Heather." He rubbed his chin with his right hand. "We have them waiting for you."

Druxin fingered his beard. "This gets more exciting each day." He curled his lip. "I love seeing how these Humans squeal when being tormented by my Krogs." He stood up. "Lead me to them. They'll tell me where Ordway and Heather are or else."

Maddock led him to where the four squires were imprisoned. He motioned to the door. "They're in there." He paused. "I must warn you they're just thirteen or fourteen year-old squires, but one of them is the lad of Duke Wilbur, Prince Ordway's cousin."

"Duke Wilbur? He and his wife Duchess Bernia are part of the Oralee visitors." He snickered. "This should prove to be quite interesting."

Maddock opened the door and gestured for Druxin to go ahead of him. Druxin immediately threw a ball of fire against the far wall causing the squires to jump with terror. Next, he shot a bolt of lightning nearly touching the arm of one of them. "Now, do any of you want to tell me where Prince Ordway and Princess Ardith Heather are?"

By this time the squires were all huddled in a corner of the room with pallid faces. In a shrill voice, one of them spoke. "We don't know. They weren't in the castle." His voice lowered to a whisper. "All of us were attending the annual Squire Tournament."

"Who are you lad?" Druxin said, eyes glaring.

"I'm Squire Robert, sir." He said, his voice trembling.

"Does anyone know more than that?" Druxin said, sending a bolt of lightning over Squire Robert's head.

"When we returned, they were all gone." Another said, through quivering lips.

"I asked for more information." Druxin said, shooting a ball of fire that consumed a wooden bucket in front of a squire's feet. "And who are you?"

"Sir, I'm Squire Alfred," he said, his face turning pallid.

Druxin shot another bolt of lightening over their heads. "Which one of you is Duke Wilbur's lad?"

A squire stood up and wiped the sweat off his forehead with his right hand. "I'm Lord Joshua, Duke Wilbur's youngest lad." His voice started to tremble. "H-have you killed him?"

Druxin shot a bolt of lightening across the room. "Yes! If you don't tell me where the others are, you will follow."

Lord Joshua fell to the floor and let out an uncontrollable cry. He took several quick breaths and stood up. "How can I tell you what I don't know?" He closed his eyes. "I guess you had better kill me."

Druxin's lip curled up, and he threw a ball of fire over the heads of the other three. "Which one of you has information of the whereabouts of Prophet Godric, Prophetess Edith, Prince Ordway, Princess Ardith Heather, Sir Richard Oswald, Lady Dawn, Sir Anthony Rice, Lady Roselee, or Sir Archibald Godwin?"

A red-haired squire stood up, hugging himself tightly. "I'm Squire Marvin, and we were hoping you could tell us where they are." He stepped forward, trembling. "I mean, they all used to take trips, but we never knew where they went."

Lord Joshua nodded his head. "Perhaps, they're all on one of those trips." He wiped the sweat off his forehead with his right hand. "The trips usually lasted about a month or so." He paused. "It's been about that long, so they should be back any day."

"Yes, that's right." Squire Marvin said, nodding his head.

Druxin motioned for Maddock to follow him out. After Maddock shut the door, Druxin shot a ball of fire at some Humans walking in a nearby field. "I was so intent on finding you, I forgot about them being in Oralee when I left."

Maddock's gray eyes bulged. "You mean they're in Oralee?"

"Well, we haven't found any trace of them here." Druxin gave an evil snicker. "But I did lay a few surprises around while I was gathering information about you. I know they don't have any power over what I've prepared for them." He fingered his beard. "I believe we'll get busy training our army. The viler we can make them, the more powerful they'll become."

"What about the four squires?"

"Let them go." Druxin said, cupping his hands. "I believe they're too afraid to be of consequences to us. Besides, they may prove to be quite beneficial later on." He fingered his beard with his right hand. "If we eliminate all who disagree with us, who will be our servants?" He gestured with his right hand. "After all, we don't want to do manual tasks ourselves."

Maddock smirked. "Your cunning knows no end. It was a remarkable day when I found you in Oralee."

"I've never forgotten the advice you gave me in the beginning." Druxin said, fingering his black beard. "You said evil has no conscience." His eyes gleamed. "That motto has served me well."

After Griffin warned Master Godric and Sir Richard not to go forward, Godric immediately stopped and allowed the Elfdins to go ahead according to their supernatural power. Mistress Meredith and Master Drew, Catrin and Griffin, Dylan, Rhonda and Owen, Patrick and Winifred, David and Meghan, Gwent and Gwendolyn, Archer and Kevyn, Falconer and Heidi, and Fletcher and Ariana.

Catrin waved her right hand up in the air. "Listen up! The evil is just ahead. We must be on the alert."

Dylan felt his stomach tighten. "I sense an evil greater than anything we have undergone since we left Oralee."

Griffin prayed. "Sovereign God! We need direction from you. Your word says *my grace is sufficient for thee: for my strength is made perfect in weakness.* You are our power, and we intreat you for the strength to stand against whatever is ahead. I ask in your name."

"Amen!" They all said in unison.

Suddenly, their horses began to snort and refused to go forward. Godric motioned to the others. "The horses sense the danger. They'll not go forward." He pointed left to a clearing in the distant trees. "Let's tie them to those trees." He dismounted. "After we've taken care of what is ahead, we can remount them."

Griffin shook his head. "Master Godric, you and Sir Richard cannot proceed with us. Both of you must stay with the horses." He paused. "We need you to take us to the others. It's more important for you to stay safe."

"I understand." Godric said, his six foot stature drooping. "It's just that I always lead, but I sense the Sovereign God is directing this."

Sir Richard nodded his head. "I may be trained to do physical combat, but I have no training against the supernatural evil of Druxin."

Master Drew rubbed his chin with his right hand. "Okay, warriors, it's time to move forward."

Mistress Meredith grabbed his left arm with her right hand. "We have to wait." She gestured towards Catrin with her right hand. "What is it?"

Catrin's eyebrows scrunched together. "I don't know how to say this, but we can't all proceed." She gestured with both hands and shrugged her shoulders. "I believe that Griffin, myself, Master Drew, Mistress Meredith, Dylan, Owen, and Rhonda are to stand side by side. Dylan is to be in the middle with Master Drew on his left, Mistress Meredith on his right, Griffin and I on Mistress Meredith's right and Owen and Rhonda on Master Drew's left. Then we move forward." She paused. "All the rest of you are to wait until I tell you it's safe to proceed."

Patrick rubbed his temple with his right hand. "If Catrin says it, it must be so."

"Godspeed to you all." Godric said, brushing his blond curls back with his right hand.

Griffin took a deep breath. "Okay, warriors, let's do this."

As they walked several yards forward, they disappeared. Suddenly, Mistress Meredith screamed. "I can't see. My eyes are on fire."

"What in Oralee is it?" Dylan said, covering his eyes. "It's scorching my eyes."

"I can't see. My eyes are burning." Master Drew said, covering his eyes with both hands."

Back in Oralee, Sir Archibald Godwin, known as Old Chronicler, sat down near one of the arches soaring to a hundred-foot vault. He was mesmerized by the large stained-glass windows of golden yellow, brilliant ruby red, and sapphire blue framed in the arches. His attention was diverted to the altar area with smaller windows of only golden yellow below the multi-colored ones that seemed to shine like the noonday sun on the beautiful carved archway shaped like a cross. The gold lining the archway lit up like the sun itself.

As he stared at the archway, he sensed to look at the large figurines of Humans on the right. His eyes followed the shape of the cross shining brilliantly on the first figurine of the Humans. He shook his head. "Lordy me! Am I seeing things or is that some sort of door?"

He stood up and walked over to the figurine and felt to see if it could be opened. As he fidgeted with it, his fingers could feel a crack. He jerked it ajar. His mouth dropped and his hazel eyes bulged as he beheld the contents behind the door. "What are all these little gold crosses with gold chains? What are they for? How come no one mentioned these before?"

As he took out a cross with its gold chain attached, he noticed some old parchments behind. "Lordy me! What are these?" He said, his hands trembling as he opened the first parchment. "This is hundreds of years old."

Old looked around for more light. He quickly sat to read what it said. "Lordy me!" He said, his heart fluttering. "The Sovereign God made these for us Humans to wear around our necks enabling us to have supernatural power like the Elfdins." He clasped his hands together. "They'll only give power to the Humans who believe in his finished work on the cross."

"This is amazing." He said, gathering the other parchments, and sitting back to read them. "These crosses and parchments were put here hundreds of years before I entered Oralee." His lips vibrated as he blew out air. "Whoever it was, must have had no idea what the Sovereign God was talking about. How was he supposed to know what a Human was?" He threw back his head and let out a peal of laughter. "I can still remember my excitement at finding the gold cross with instructions to go to a certain place and walk straight ahead. Next thing I knew I was in another world occupied by little people dressed in forest green attire who were filled with supernatural power." He grabbed his head with both hands. "Lordy me! If we had known these gold crosses were to replace the ones we had, Maddock could not have gotten into Oralee with my nephew Richard's cross to bring evil." He stood up and paced back and forth. "How am I to get the crosses to Master Godric and the others? With Evil Druxin and Maddock conjuring up all sorts of evil, they need these crosses." He held up a cross. "One of these crosses will give them supernatural power like the Elfdins. No evil from our world will be able to overpower any who are wearing one of these gold crosses." He paused. "Of course, the Elfdins would since they're supernatural beings." He brushed his white hair back with his hands. "That's why they're in our world. Only they can destroy Druxin and his evil power."

David's eyebrows scrunched together. "What's happening? Where did they go? All I hear is screaming!" He gestured towards Patrick. "We've got to do something."

"We must do what Catrin said." Patrick rubbed his forehead with both hands. "She believed the Sovereign God was leading. If we interfere, we could make matters worse."

"Winifred shook her head. "As her Ma, I want to run right in there. But the Sovereign God has been teaching us his ways for the past two years. The Bible says, *for my thoughts are not your thoughts, neither are your ways my ways.*" She paused. "After all, it was Catrin to whom the Sovereign God first spoke."

"Besides," Archer said, "we are to *trust in the Lord with all thine heart; and lean not unto thine own understanding.* We must trust the Sovereign God has things in control."

Gwent looked David in the eyes. "Remember what Griffin said before we started out on this Crusade, '*He shall not be afraid of evil tidings: his heart is fixed, trusting in the Lord.*' We must trust in the Sovereign God."

Meghan twisted her hands. "I remember what it was like for Griffin and me when we were up in a tree not far from David and Catrin. Krogs were all around them. It was obvious they thought David and Catrin were easy prey." Meghan's eyes widened. "Suddenly, Griffin cried out in a loud voice, 'Sovereign God! Please hear me. I'm Griffin, the future great prophet of the Elfdins. I don't know you, but my high prince said you are supposed to dispel evil. Krogs are as evil as they come. Meghan and I are powerless to help Catrin and David. I ask you to deliver the heirs of my high prince from the horrible beasts.'" She paused. "After Griffin prayed, the Pundles came to their rescue." Her eyes filled with tears. "I believe we need to pray."

Master Godric's face screwed up. "I don't know what's happening to me. This whole thing has me flabbergasted. My world is a war zone. Evil is destroying it." He threw up both hands. "As we stand in the whole armor of God, we are to be *praying always with all prayer and supplication in the Spirit, and watching thereunto with all perseverance and supplication for all saints.*" He blew out a heavy sigh. "My grandmother always told me evil has no conscience, but prayer is greater than any evil." He grabbed his head with both hands. "Where's my faith. Only supernatural faith will disable evil. We need to quench the enemy's fiery darts through prayer."

Chapter 4

Light Dissipates Darkness

CATRIN FELT HER LEGS shake as she heard Dylan, Mistress Meredith, and Drew all screaming. Suddenly, she knew what to do. "Darkness can't comprehend light." She said, throwing a ball of fire lighting up the place.

Griffin grasped what she was doing and followed with a ball of fire. "Owen! Rhonda! Follow us with more balls of fire."

As Griffin, Rhonda, and Owen continued to throw the balls of fire, Catrin laid her hands on Mistress Meredith's eyes. Immediately, she was healed and reached to lay hands on Drew while Catrin laid hands on Dylan.

"Okay!" Catrin said. "Everyone continue to blast that evil with the balls of fire. It's crumbling."

Owen gestured with both hands. "Affirmative! It's dissipated."

"Indubitably!" Rhonda said, shooting her left fist into the air.

Griffin fell to his knees. "Thank the Sovereign God for his intervening."

Catrin punched the air with her right hand. "Our Sovereign God is awesome!"

"Undeniably." Dylan said, sighing heavily. "What manner of malevolence was that?"

Griffin scratched the back of his head with his right hand. "No wonder the Sovereign God wanted us to come here. Humans have no supernatural power to combat such wickedness."

"I wonder what else Druxin has done to this world?" Drew said, rubbing his chin with his right hand.

Mistress Meredith gave Catrin a hug. "Again, we really must remember the power of his word." She gazed into Catrin's emerald eyes. "I may be the Great Prophetess, but it's obvious your yielding to the Sovereign God has enabled you to be more powerful."

Catrin hung her head. "I don't think I'm more powerful. It's just the power of his word." She shrugged her shoulders. "I heard *the light shineth in darkness; and the darkness comprehended it not.*" She gestured with both hands. "I knew darkness can't overcome the supernatural light of the Sovereign God." She paused. "I just obeyed." She gazed at each of them gesturing with both hands. "After that, you all did the same thing."

Master Drew's eyebrows scrunched together. "I believe Catrin's right. It's not about being more powerful. It's a matter of being more sensitive to the Sovereign God and his word which says, *for I say, through the grace given unto me, to every man that is among you, not to think of himself more highly than he ought to think; but to think soberly, according as God hath dealt to every man the measure of faith.*" He gestured towards Catrin and Griffin. "Because they are more sensitive to the Sovereign God's word, they have strengthened their measure of faith through believing his word." He rubbed his chin with his right hand. "Now, we have to start standing on his word and not our combat training."

"Sensitivity to the Sovereign God's word facilitates his power." Rhonda said, fidgeting with her left earlobe.

Dylan nodded his head. "We expended copious years utilizing natural warfare. Now we need to neglect the natural and surrender to the supernatural power of our God." He motioned towards Catrin and Griffin. "The younger generation are more guided by the Sovereign God, because they expended fewer years utilizing natural means."

"That's why the measure of faith given to them has been strengthened." Meredith said, nodding her head. "We need to trust in his word and not our natural ability if our faith is to be fortified."

"Phenomenal!" Rhonda said.

"Oh my!" Catrin said, grabbing her head with both hands. "Let me tell the others it's safe."

Dewey Ryn was busy molding the warriors on the mountain into warbands. "This is so strange." He said, chuckling. "After all the years of using bows and arrows to be hitting targets with bolts of lightning is incredible." He motioned with both hands for everyone to stop. "Okay, we need to become efficient enough to hit the bullseye the first time."

As he was speaking, one of the warriors shouted. "A Krog's coming up the mountain!"

Dewey turned, looked down the mountain, and saw a Krog climbing towards them. "Sovereign God! Please help us. What do we do? How did he come through the invisible wall? If we attack it, Druxin will know we're here." He felt his heart racing. "Do what?" He motioned to everyone. "Just stand next to each other to hide our camp, the caves, the Pundles, and say, *but thou, O Lord, art a shield for me.*"

Everyone stood in front of the camp and said, "*But thou, O Lord, art a shield for me.*"

They watched as the Krog climbed and came closer. Once it was several yards from the Elfdins, it stopped, sniffed, and looked around. After a few moments, it turned around, climbed back down the mountain, and disappeared from sight.

Dewey stumbled back a step. "We weren't seen."

Rowena, his wife, ran to hug him. "How did you know to do that?"

Dewey gave a blank look. "When I prayed, I heard that Jesus *passing through the midst of them went his way.* Then I felt to tell everyone to say, *but thou, O Lord, art a shield for me.*" He gestured with both hands. "I'm in shock."

Rowena gave out a huge breath. "It seems like the Sovereign God has given us more supernatural power than what we are aware of in this world."

"Well, this is a natural world, ours is a supernatural world."
He gestured with both hands. "Besides, this world may be the
world we have to remain in." He shrugged his shoulders. "We have
no gold crosses to get back to Oralee."

Kimball, Rowena's brother scratched the back of his head
with his right hand. "How come we can see each other, but the
Krog didn't see us?"

Dewey grabbed his head with both hands. "That's a good
question!" His face screwed up. "I think the Sovereign God wants
us to comprehend he's our shield against evil."

"Also, we need to realize the power of his word." Rowena said,
holding her face with both hands.

"What made the Krog come up the mountain?" Kimball said,
his eyebrows knitting together.

Dewey gestured with both hands. "He may have spotted the
bolts of lightning."

Rowena's eyebrows scrunched together. "Does that mean our
bolts of lightning are now invisible?"

"I don't believe our bolts are shielded." Dewey said, smiling.
"The Sovereign God is our shield."

Druxin and Maddock gathered all the evil apprentices for further
training in dark powers by revealing how to be possessed by the
vile forces known as demons. Druxin threw a few bolts of lightning over their heads. They all ran in different directions. "Get
back here." He said. "If you want to learn, you have to see what you
can be capable of." He watched as they all took their previous place.
"The first thing you have to be aware of is evil has no conscience.
If you are concerned about hurting someone, you can go back to
your rooms."

Maddock's gray eyes squinted. "What are you saying?"

Druxin motioned with his right hand for Maddock to be
silent.

As two left their place and walked away, Druxin struck them
both with a bolt of lightening sending them to the ground unable

to move or speak. "They can stay there until we finish our lesson." He said, snickering.

He walked towards one of the apprentices with raven black hair and emerald eyes. "What's your name?"

"Arthur, sir."

Druxin chortled and motioned for Arthur to step forward. "I believe you shall be my star pupil." He laid his hands upon his head. "Receive the power of the evil one."

Immediately, Arthur's eyes glared, he fell backwards on his back, and his hands shot several bolts of lightning up into the air.

"Get up!" Druxin said. "Now, you lay your hands on the heads of your fellow evil prophets and say what I said."

As Arthur laid his hands on each one, their eyes glared. When he finished, he gestured towards Druxin. "How come they aren't falling backwards and shooting bolts of lightning?"

"They will learn, but you will be the most powerful of them."

Maddock's gray eyes squinted. "Are you going to lay hands on my head?"

"Arthur and I are both going to lay hands on your head. You will be more powerful than them all." He cupped his hands. "I owe you much for introducing me to the dark power." He gestured towards Arthur. "Okay, we must lay our hands on Maddock." They both laid hands on Maddock's head, and Druxin said, "Receive the power of the evil one."

Maddock's gray eyes glared, fell backwards, and he shot a ball of fire that Druxin immediately stopped. "You almost destroyed some of our pupils." Druxin said, snickering.

Maddock shook his head. "This is amazing. I never dreamed I could possess such power."

"Okay, all of you form a straight line over there." Druxin pointed towards his right. "You see that rock? That's where you're going to practice throwing bolts of lightning." He paused. "Not Maddock and Arthur. You both may destroy it before the others learn how to do it."

Catrin quickly turned to dispel the shroud that prevented the others from seeing what was happening. With a wave of her hand, it crackled like fire and disappeared.

Griffin shook his head. "How in Oralee did you do that?"

Catrin's eyebrows scrunched together. "The Sovereign God told me to do it."

Before she could say more, David ran to them. "What happened? Why were you screaming? How did you disappear?"

Griffin scratched the back of his head with his right hand. "It had to be an evil put here by Druxin to stop the Humans. All we know is it tried to blind my Pa, my Ma, and Dylan." He pointed towards Catrin. "She heard the Sovereign God tell her light dispels darkness."

Rhonda shook both fists. "It was astounding! They were screaming, but Catrin hurled balls of fire illuminating the place."

"Griffin followed suit and instructed us to do likewise." Owen said. "Then Catrin laid hands on Mistress Meredith, then Mistress Meredith laid hands on Master Drew, and Catrin laid hands on my Pa." He grabbed his head with both hands. "It was phenomenal!"

Master Drew rubbed his chin with his right hand. "The more light that generated, the more the dark spell dissolved."

"Darkness cannot vanquish light." Rhonda said, doing a two-step.

Patrick ran his fingers along the scar from his right temple to his chin. "I just knew we had to trust Catrin's sensitivity to the Sovereign God."

David clasped his hands together. "I was ready to run in there and help, but Ma and Pa stopped me." He gestured towards Archer. "He reminded me to not lean on my own understanding."

Winifred hugged her lass. "Believe me, Catrin, it took a lot for me to not run in there, but I knew the Sovereign God has been teaching us his ways. We had to trust him and not get in his way."

Meghan twisted her hands. "I remembered when you and David were up in a tree surrounded by Krogs. Griffin and I were powerless to help. When Griffin prayed to the Sovereign God, help came." She shuffled her feet and looked down. "I just knew we had to pray."

Godric gave a heavy sigh. "It should have been me suggesting we pray, but this whole thing has me quite unsettled." He paused. "I always teach the light of God's word will always dissipate darkness. Prayer is where we do our major spiritual warfare." He hung his head. "I don't understand this evil of Druxin, or why I seem to be impotent. But I will obey the Sovereign God and stay back."

"Wait a minute!" Griffin said. "There's something going on with Old Chronicler."

Catrin's eyebrows scrunched together. "One of us must get to him quickly." She paused. "It has to be Rhonda."

Rhonda fidgeted with her left earlobe. "I undeniably concur."

Master Godric took Old's gold cross out of his saddlebag. "You'll need this to get in to see him."

Owen gestured with both hands. "I must attend her."

Catrin nodded her head. "I believe the Sovereign God usually sends them out by twos." She paused. "How will they know how to find us when they return?"

Archer scratched the back of his head with his right hand. "We'll do what our ancestors did at first when hunting until they knew their way around the Ravine outside the perimeter of the gold crosses." He gestured with both hands. "We'll use stones to point the way. Two light stones side by side and a dark one in the middle directing the way to go."

"Brilliant!" Owen said.

Old Chronicler was amazed at the information on the parchments he found hidden with the miniature gold crosses on gold chains. "Oh, Lordy me! Sovereign God, I need to get this information to the Elfdins and my fellow humans." His lips vibrated as he blew out air. "I must be patient. You are more aware of what is needed than I am." He sat back and laughed. "Thank you for having me stay behind. If you hadn't led me to that hidden door, it might have been hundreds of years before this was known." He clasped his hands together. "This is more exciting than when I was knighted. I can't wait to see what it'll be like to have the supernatural power of the Elfdins in my world."

He stiffened as he heard the Portal opening. His mind reeled, should he hide, or should he try the power of the cross of the Sovereign God? "I'll stand in the power of this gold cross." He said, standing tall.

As he stood firm, Rhonda came running through. "Old! Are you healthy?"

"Lordy me! Yes." He threw back his head and let out a peal of laughter. "I was just asking the Sovereign God how I can get some vital information to the Elfdins and my fellow humans, when you come running through the Portal."

Rhonda's face screwed up. "Critical intelligence?"

Old reached into his tunic and pulled out the little gold cross hanging on a gold chain around his neck. "This enables us to have supernatural power like you." He paused. "Of course, because Elfdins are supernatural, you will be more powerful. However, we will be a formidable power against evil."

Rhonda shot her left fist up in the air. "Astounding!" She gave him a hug. "This is going to be needed by the Humans out there to fight the evil of Druxin and Maddock." She paused. "There was a terrible evil that tried to blind Master Drew, Mistress Meredith, and Dylan." She gestured with her left hand. "It was Catrin who comprehended light dissipates darkness and had me, Owen, and Griffin follow her with balls of fire." She did a two-step. "It was prodigious!"

Old gestured with both hands. "There's more. The Elfdins don't need gold crosses to get back. This is your world, and you can just go in and out." He paused. "However, these little gold crosses are all we need to get in." He clasped his hands together. "If someone steals it, it won't work. Once it's on us, its supernatural power becomes part of us. That's the power of the cross of the Sovereign God. It's amazing!" He shook his head. "If we had been in possession of these crosses, evil Maddock would never have entered Oralee." He threw up his hands. "Only those who believe in his finished work on the cross will have his supernatural power with these crosses."

"Wow! That is astounding." She shot her left fist up in the air. "I should depart. Owen is waiting outside the Portal."

Old ran and grabbed his backpack and handed Rhonda a satchel full of gold crosses. "We need to get these little crosses to Master Godric and the others who have accepted the Sovereign God's finished work on the cross." He laughed. "If someone who doesn't believe tries to enter Oralee, the crosses will be nothing more than a trinket." He grabbed his head with both hands. "Lordy me! I almost forgot. Once all the Elfdins entered my world, the time difference ended. Now, we can both go in and out of our worlds and the time is the same." He threw his head back and gave out a peal of laughter. "That's why I've only aged several days since you left."

"Wait a minute!" Rhoda said. "You should continue here for protection."

Old pulled out the gold cross. "I have this. Because of this cross, I have supernatural power." He clasped his hands together. "Lordy me! Haven't you heard anything I said? I now possess supernatural power from the Sovereign God. He's all the protection I need." He pointed to Pearl and Pemberton, his Pundles. "They'll come with me. I'm fonder of them than I realized."

Herald Roth's eyes widened as he saw Owen and Rhonda approaching the Portal. Before he could get there, Rhonda went through. "Owen!" He said. "What are you two doing? Is something wrong? Where are the others?"

Owen combed his ash blond hair back with his fingers. "Griffin and Catrin discerned Rhonda should get to Old swiftly."

"Oh my! I do hope he's fine."

Before Owen could respond, Old, Rhonda, Pearl, and Pemberton came through the Portal.

Owen gestured with both hands. "Old! What are you undertaking? You stated the Sovereign God wanted you to remain in Oralee."

"Lordy me! Listen up, future spiritual mentor, I'm about to experience the supernatural power of the cross of the Sovereign God." He reached into his tunic with his right hand and pulled out the little gold cross hanging from the gold chain around his neck. "I found a hidden door in the Gold Temple. Behind it were thousands of gold crosses on gold chains and several parchments of information." He clasped his hands together. "I believe I was to stay behind to find these crosses and the parchments." He put the cross back under his tunic. "Once we humans put on this cross, the supernatural power of the cross of the Sovereign God becomes ours. There's much more, but I'll wait until I get to the others and tell all."

Rhonda interrupted him. "Plus, a cross is not necessitated for Elfdins to return to Oralee."

Old's eyes caught sight of two ponies. "Lordy me!" He laughed. "You two have learned how to ride." He clasped his hands. "Let me call Saber, my horse. He always stays close by when I go into Oralee. There's a huge grazing area near a lake where I built a shed for him to stay." He put his right thumb and forefinger into his mouth and gave out a shrill whistle. "Keep your eyes focused on the woods to the right." As they watched the woods, a beautiful white stallion came running towards them. "That's my boy." He paused. "Lordy me! I do wish he could come with me into Oralee." His eyebrows scrunched together. "Since things are changed, I believe he can come with me."

Saber ran over to Old and nuzzled his nose against Old's right shoulder. "I've missed you too, my boy."

Pearl and Pemberton began to bark. "It's okay you two." Old said. "This here is like a son to me." He rubbed Saber's neck. "His father, Blade, was given to me when I was twenty-five and died when I was sixty. Saber has been with me ten years now." His eyes teared. "He's been a blessing from the Sovereign God." He threw his head back and let out a peal of laughter. "With this cross, I feel like Caleb about to go into the promise land and subdue the Canaanites."

Rhonda's face screwed up. "I detect an urgency to proceed."

"Unequivocally!" Owen said.

Herald Roth scratched the back of head with his left hand. "I'm not sure if I'm supposed to stay here with Old leaving."

Rhonda's face screwed up. "The necessity appears to be negated."

"Perhaps you can put your belongings on your Pundle and ride with Owen." Old said.

Rhonda, Owen, and Herald loaded his belongings on Taffy's back. "Splendid!" Owen said. "Currently, sit with me, and let us proceed."

Chapter 5

Right Place At The Right Time

DRUXIN GAZED AT THE two lying on the ground. "I think I'll leave them for the vultures." He snickered. "First, let them die a slow agonizing death." He pointed towards a wooded area in the distance. "Put them in there. I don't want them interfering with our training."

As four of Maddock's apprentices rushed to pick the two up, Druxin curled his lip. "Those four will be Squires over all the apprentices." He fingered his black beard with his right hand. "I think I'll be Grand Master Druxin, then Marshall Maddock, Knight Arthur, the four Squires, and all the others will be apprentices in that order." He chortled. "We'll be called the knights of vile power."

Maddock rubbed his hands together. "We'll rule this world, and no one will be able to stop us." He sneered. "Never did I dream of such renown. We'll be feared by all."

Arthur's emerald eyes beamed. "I have a few people I'd like to visit with my power. They thought I wasn't good enough to join them in play as children." His nostrils flared. "I'll show them just how good I am."

Druxin curled his lip. "I can relate to not being good enough. I'm still working on my revenge." He snickered. "You go take care of yours." He pointed towards the four carrying the two to the woods. "Take the Squires with you." He waited for the four to return. "I'll have you lay hands on them again to give them a little extra power." He fingered his black beard with his right hand. "I'll send Soot with you. She's enough to frighten any human."

Arthur laid his hands on the four sergeants. "Receive an extra increase of evil power."

Immediately their eyes glared, they fell backward, and each shot a bolt of lightning. "Wow!" Arthur said. "I'll have a most formidable army with me."

"What are their names?" Druxin said.

Arthur pointed to each one. "The redhead is Elton, the stocky blond is Winter, the thin blond is Hollie, and the brawny one is Oxford."

"Old! Is something erroneous with my horse? It's hobbling." Rhonda said, her eyebrows drawing together.

"Lordy me! I do believe it lost its shoe." He gazed around. "There's a small town a short ways from here. My second cousin is the blacksmith." He shook his head. "You'll have to ride with me, and we'll hold the reins for your horse to stay with us."

Rhonda fidgeted with her left earlobe. "I dislike deviating from our destination, but I don't choose to afflict my horse."

She dismounted, handed Old her reins, and he helped her climb up behind him. "You take the reins." He gestured towards Herald Roth. "We'll move a little slower, so we don't put too much pressure on the horse to keep up."

They moved along and kept watch on Rhonda's horse. "Is it considerably further?" Owen said, his eyebrows squishing together.

"It's a little ways." Old said. "When we get out of these woods, there's a clearing, and the town's past the next woods."

"Great Jehoshaphat!" Rhonda said, her face screwing up. "Something's ahead. We ought to dismount and walk."

Owen gestured with his left hand. "I perceive objects adjacent to the rock beyond that cluster of trees."

They dismounted and Rhonda gazed at Old. "You and Herald remain with the horses. Owen and I will proceed."

As Owen and Rhonda entered the woods, they spotted two figures lying on the ground near the rock. Rhonda quickly ran to them with Owen right behind. "It's two humans!" Rhonda said. "They're paralyzed."

Owen combed his ash blond hair back with his fingers. "Undeniably the work of Druxin."

Old heard them and ran their way with Herald following behind. "Lordy me! That's my second cousin, Chester's lad, Matthew." He scratched the back of his head with his right hand. "I have no idea who the girl is."

Rhonda's face screwed up. "Old, does Matthew trust in the Sovereign God? Does he believe he died on the cross for his sins, was buried, and rose from the dead?"

"He did." Old said, shaking his head. "But I don't know why he's dressed like one of Maddock's apprentices."

"Regarding the gold crosses, aren't they designed to provide believing humans supernatural power?" Rhonda said, fidgeting with her left earlobe.

"Lordy me! You're right."

"I consider placing a gold cross about each neck." She said, matter-of-factly. "If their heart receives it, the supernatural power of the cross of the Sovereign God will restore."

Owen ran to Saber, retrieved a few crosses from Old's saddlebag, hurried back, and handed them to him. As soon as Old put the cross around their necks, they each sat up.

"Cousin Archibald!" Matthew said. "How did you find us? What did you do to heal us?"

Old's lips vibrated as he blew out air. "The question to be answered is what are you both doing here?"

Matthew hung his head. "I got caught up in wanting to be one of Maddock's apprentices. I thought evil was cool." His eyes teared. "This malicious guy, called Druxin, said evil has no conscience. If we were concerned about hurting someone, we could go back to our rooms." He gestured towards the girl. "Ivey and I have people we love very much and wouldn't want to hurt them."

Ivey interrupted. "As we walked away, Druxin hit us with something that paralyzed us." She began to shake all over. "He said we were to be left to die and would be food for the vultures."

"That sounds like Druxin, alright." Herald said, shaking his head.

Rhonda shot her left fist up in the air. "Thank the Sovereign God for having us in the right place at the right time!" She did a two-step. "You are flourishing and possess supernatural power from him."

"Cousin Archibald, how did you mend us?"

"Lordy me! It wasn't me. It was the Sovereign God." He gestured towards the gold crosses around their neck. "The power of the Sovereign God's cross is what healed you."

"The Sovereign God's supernatural capability is phenomenal!" Owen said.

"Wait a minute!" Matthew said, gazing at Rhonda. "Did you say we have supernatural power from the Sovereign God?" His eyebrows squished together. "We joined Maddock to receive evil power. Why would the Sovereign God gives us his power?"

Owen combed his ash blond hair back with his fingers. "When you departed Druxin and Maddock, you advanced towards the Sovereign God."

"Your heart transmuted from malevolence to virtue." Rhonda said.

Ivey's eyes widened. "Who are you little people?" She paused. "You are dressed in forest green like evil Druxin and about his size."

Old clasped his hands together. "Ivey, these are Elfdins from a far away land who possess supernatural power from the Sovereign God." His lips vibrated as he blew out air. "Their status in their supernatural land enables them to possess powers greater than ours." He paused. "Druxin comes from their land, but he allowed Maddock to influence him to dark power. That's why he seems to be more powerful here."

"Since we are from a supernatural land, we all possess more power in this natural land." Herald said, scratching the back of his head with his left hand.

"I think I have a confession to make." Ivey said, hanging her head. "With this gold cross, I cannot continue in a lie."

"A falsehood?" Rhonda said, her face screwing up.

"Yes. My name is not Ivey. I made it up to join Maddock." She let out a heavy sigh. "My name is Mary. I was named after my mother, and she loved the Sovereign God." Her eyes filled with tears. "I hated him for taking her, but I couldn't follow Maddock using her name."

"Plus, that name is the name of the Sovereign God's mother." Old said, giving her a hug.

"I don't know what's happening." Mary said, her eyebrows scrunching together. "I believe I need to have another gold cross. It's not for me." She gestured with both hands. "I just know it's imperative for me to have another one."

"Precisely." Rhonda said, fidgeting with her left earlobe. "It's extremely peculiar, but accurate."

"I'll not argue with the Sovereign God." Old said, handing another gold cross to Mary.

"I'm to wear it with the cross hanging on my back." Mary said, putting it on. "It'll have no power upon me, but I am not to lose it."

"I perceive we should progress to that town." Rhonda said.

Owen nodded his head. "Precisely!"

Matthew hung his head. "I had a terrible row with my father about leaving."

"If I know your father, he's waiting with open arms for his prodigal lad." Old said.

"That has always been his favorite Bible story. He said many times, if God could forgive him for what he did, he should always welcome any prodigal from the faith back with open arms." Matthew's eyes filled with tears. "It looks like it's me."

Knight Arthur, Squires Elton, Hollie, Winter, Oxford, along with Soot headed for their destination. Arthur's nostrils enlarged. "This is the day I'll go down in history for destroying those prigs who thought I wasn't good enough for them." He clenched his teeth.

"Said I was too interested in evil." He stood tall, chin forward. "Now, I'm the third most powerful person in the world." He gave a guttural chortle. "I'll especially enjoy torturing my father, the vicar, who said I'd turn out no good if I didn't change my ways."

Elton's mouth widened into a grin. "Who would have believed we'd be this mighty?" He punched the air with his right fist. "I'm ready to take on the world."

Winter nodded her head. "I don't have any revenge that I know of, but I'll help Knight Arthur accomplish his."

Arthur put up his right hand. "Everyone be quiet. Once we exit these woods, the town is there." His eyes glared. "This day has been long in coming, but it'll be such sweet revenge on the believers in the Sovereign God and his stupid cross that's impotent."

Soot's mouth formed a grin. "That's my girl." Arthur said, patting her head. "I think I'll let you go in front of us." His emerald eyes beamed. "The sight of you will have them all running. Then, we'll throw a few lightning bolts." He gazed at the others, firmly. "We don't want to destroy them quickly. I want them on their knees pleading for their life."

Oxford rubbed his hands together. "My heart is pounding out of my chest. I've never felt so exhilarated in my life."

Hollie looked down at the ground. "What about the children and the elderly?"

Arthur's face reddened and his eyes glowed. "What do you mean?"

"I was wondering if we might spare them. After all, what can they do against us?" She gestured with both hands. "They can't use physical strength to combat us. What pleasure is there in that?"

Arthur got up in her face. "You were warned that evil has no conscience. You had your opportunity to walk away with Matthew and Ivey."

"I didn't walk away because I want to be part of the knights of vile power."

"Then, you'll do as I say. Right?" Arthur said, his teeth clenching.

"Yes." She said, looking away.

The Crusade moved along towards the castle hidden in the old forest where Mistress Edith, High Prince Ordway, High Princess Ardith Heather, Lady Dawn Oswald, and the others were safely hidden from Druxin and Maddock.

"We're getting closer to the old forest." Godric said. "I do hope we don't encounter any more of Druxin's traps."

"Are they in the castle or hiding in the cavern?" Archer said, scratching the back of his head with his right hand.

"Wait a minute!" Catrin said, her eyebrows scrunching together. "I'm feeling that Owen and Rhonda are heading into trouble."

"I agree." Griffin said, his eyebrows scrunching together. "I believe they'll need our help."

Dylan screwed up his face. "They are highly formidable in opposition to any evil."

"It's not that. I believe it's the onslaught of evil about to confront them." Catrin said.

"What do we do?" Patrick said, rubbing his forehead with both hands.

"Griffin and I must go help them." Catrin said, matter-of-factly.

"I'm going with you two." David said. "If the onslaught is to be that powerful, we need to be ready for it."

"All I know is that I'm to join you three." Meghan said, twisting her hands.

Griffin scratched the back of his head with his right hand. "How do we find them?"

"*I will instruct thee and teach thee in the way which thou shalt go: I will guide thee with mine eye.*" Catrin said, gesturing with both hands. "I believe the Sovereign God will guide the horses to them."

Mistress Meredith closed her eyes and rubbed her forehead with her right hand. "They must leave quickly."

"I'm glad we know the Sovereign God." Winifred said, sighing heavily. "I want to join them, but I'll trust him."

"We'll just continue to leave our trail, but I sense we have to get to the castle or the cavern quickly." Master Drew said, rubbing his chin with his right hand. "The sooner we're out of sight, we can regroup and get direction from the Sovereign God on how to proceed."

"Godspeed!" Godric said, as Catrin, Griffin, David, and Meghan headed towards Rhonda and Owen.

Vanora was busy teaching Michael all she knew about healing herbs. "Prophetess Christina has a collection of herbs that has made it easier for me to teach you." She said, giggling.

"Help!" Susanna said, interrupting them. "Michael's mother fell down." She gestured with both hands. "Her leg is broken." Her eyes pleaded. "She can't get up."

"Where is she?" Michael said. "I'll grab some Boswellia for the pain." He grabbed his head with both hands. "Herbs won't heal a broken leg."

"Michael, listen to me." Vanora said, touching his left arm with her right hand. "The Sovereign God is able to heal whatever." She motioned to Susanna. "Take us to her."

"Yes, yes. Follow me."

Golda was lying on the ground with her leg contorted from the break. "I broke my leg." She said, sweating profusely.

"Mother!" Michael said. "I have some Boswellia for the pain." He quickly administered it to her.

Vanora gazed at Golda. "I'm not my mother, but I possess the supernatural power of the Sovereign God." She sat on the ground next to Golda and laid hands on her. "Sovereign God you are *the Lord that healeth*. Through the power of the cross of the Sovereign God, heal Golda's leg."

Susanna and Michael glared wide-eyed as Golda's leg began to straighten. She stopped sweating and sat up. "Will you two help me up?" She put her arms up. "Will you two stop gawking and help me up?"

"Of course, mother." Michael said, shaking his head. "I just witnessed a miracle. I know the Bible talks about them, but to actually see one." He grabbed his head with both hands. "It says, *I am the Lord that healeth thee.*"

They helped Golda up. "Thank you!" Golda said, embracing Vanora.

"It was the Sovereign God, not me." She put up both palms. "It's faith in what he accomplished on the cross. The Bible says *if thou canst believe, all things are possible to him that believeth.*"

"He healed us spiritually and physically." Michael said. "*By whose stripes ye were healed.*" He said, hunching his shoulders. "How could I forget his word?"

Vanora touched his left hand with her right hand. "Believe me. I know that can happen." She rubbed her arms with both hands. "In my world, something happened because of Druxin deceiving my ancestrals." She paused. "That deceit caused us to forget about the Sovereign God and we spent 400 years without our supernatural power." She sighed heavily. "We actually forgot who the Sovereign God was."

"Druxin!" Michael said, his mouth falling open. "Isn't he the one causing destruction here?" He gestured with his hands. "You did say 400 years?" His eyebrows scrunched together. "Are you that old?"

"No!" Vanora said, giggling. "Somehow Maddock taught Druxin dark powers. With our world being supernatural, Druxin did something to live longer." Her face screwed up. "However, he can no longer get back into our world. So, I don't know if his power to live longer will cease here."

"I wish we could lay hands on people to heal them." Susanna said.

Michael scratched the back of head with his right hand. "It says *they shall lay hands on the sick, and they shall recover.*"

"Exactly!" Vanora said. "Faith is supernatural and what the Sovereign God can do through the power of faith in his word and in his supernatural power is awesome."

Michael hit his forehead with his right hand. "The Bible tells us to *take the shield of faith, wherewith ye shall be able to quench all the fiery darts of the wicked.*" He paused. "I was so busy trying to get evil power that destroys, kills, and harms. The Sovereign God's power restores, gives life, and heals." His eyes teared. "Why didn't I see evil power can do nothing good or beneficial?"

"Michael, I know the loss of your father caused you pain." Golda said. "But he was ready to meet the Sovereign God in person." Tears filled her eyes. "Before he died, he prayed for you to serve him too."

"I promise to live the rest of my life making sure my father's prayer is a reality."

Old Chronicler stopped his horse. "I think before we enter the town, I should give Matthew something different to wear." He pointed to Matthew's clothes. "That outfit may be too much for his father, my cousin, to bear."

Mary hung her head and gestured with her right hand. "I sure wish I didn't have this on."

"I wonder." Rhonda said, dismounting from Old's horse. She walked over to Mary and placed both hands on her shoulders. "Clothe in the apparel prior to enlisting with Maddock."

Immediately, Mary was clothed in a russet gown, a semi-circular cloak fastened with a cord, and leather shoes rising just above her ankle. "Oh my!" Mary said. "How did you do that? This is exactly what I was wearing the day I joined Maddock."

Matthew gestured towards Rhonda with his right hand. "Can you do that for me?"

"Wait one confounded minute!" Owen said, dismounting from his pony. "Undoubtedly, it's my turn." He placed both hands on Matthew's shoulders. "Clothe in your apparel prior to enlisting with Maddock."

Instantaneously, he was clothed in russet breeches with a drawstring, a russet tunic, and a brown hood and gorget. "This is exactly what I wore the day I joined Maddock." He turned towards Owen and Rhonda. "How did you do that?"

Owen kicked the ground with his left foot. "I'm flabbergasted."

Rhonda gestured with her left hand. "It's the Sovereign God."

"Well, I declare I'm addled." Herald said, patting Taffy on the head. "I do believe I'm excited to see what the Sovereign God will have me do."

"Lordy me!" Old said. "The power of the Sovereign God becomes more overwhelming each day."

"Whew!" Rhonda said, shooting her left fist up in the air. "This is significantly exhilarating."

Matthew, touching his gold cross looked at Owen. "Does this mean the Sovereign God's cross will enable me to do that?"

"Lordy me!" Old Chronicler said, clasping his hands together. "Owen, Rhonda, and Herald are Spiritual beings from a Spiritual world. What they are capable of will exceed the powers of Humans." He reached in his tunic and pulled out his gold cross with his right hand. "The cross of the Sovereign God gives us the power over all the power of evil."

Matthew nodded his head. "That means power over Maddock and Evil Druxin." He gave out a heavy sigh. "In truth, that's all that matters."

Old pointed to his right. "That's the entrance into the town. My cousin's forge is just ahead on the right."

"My insides are shaking like I'm on tenterhooks." Matthew said, wiping sweat from his forehead with his right hand.

Old threw back his head and let out a peal of laughter. "I do believe you have truly repented of your rebellion. Your father will be overjoyed to have his beloved lad back."

"Restrain!" Owen said. "I perceive screaming."

Rhonda nodded her head. "Humans are hysterical."

"I guess this is my time to discover what I'm capable of in this world." Herald said.

Griffin interrupted them. "We must all dismount and proceed with caution."

"W-where did you all come from?" Matthew said.

Catrin gestured with both hands. "The Sovereign God told us that Rhonda and Owen were heading into trouble. Griffin and I knew we were to help."

"That's when Meghan and I knew we were to assist." David said, nodding his head.

Once they all dismounted, Rhonda did a two-step. "He appears to conduct us to the right place at the right time."

"Wait a minute!" Meghan said, gesturing towards Old. "What are you doing here?" Her eyebrows scrunched together. "Herald! What are you doing here?" As her eyes caught sight of Matthew and Mary, she said. "Who are those two?"

"I think we had better concentrate on the source of that screaming." Griffin said, gesturing towards the town. "We can sort out who and what after we take care of whatever is happening in that town."

"My sentiments entirely." Rhonda said.

"Right." Catrin said, gesturing with both hands.

"Lordy me!" Old said, his eyebrows squishing together. "Let's tie our horses up over there in that clump of trees."

"Consider the gold crosses." Owen said, pointing to Old's saddle bag.

Old nodded his head. "I better take some of the crosses with me. There's many in that town who worship the Sovereign God. They'll need his supernatural power."

"Gold crosses?" Meghan said, her eyebrows scrunching together.

"Afterwards!" Catrin said, putting up her right hand. "Old can explain everything once we figure out what is going on in there with all that screaming."

Quickly tying up their horses, they all held hands with heads bowed. "Sovereign God." Griffin said. "We know something is going on in there, help us to stand against whatever it is. For you promise that *greater is he that is in you, than he that is in the world.*" He sighed, heavily. "We are endowed with the power of the Holy Ghost to stand against the evil day."

"Amen!" They all said in unison.

Chapter 6

Power Of The Word

MISTRESS MEREDITH'S FACE SCREWED up. "Something's wrong ahead in that clump of trees. It's another trap set up by Druxin."

Dylan nodded his head. "It is diabolical!" He felt his stomach tighten. "Mistress Meredith, Master Drew, and I are to proceed first. I am to advance with them following me." He paused. "Next will be Patrick and Winifred, then Archer and Kevyn, then Gwent and Gwendolyn, then Fletcher and Falconer, and in the rear will be Ariana and Heidi."

They all took their positions. "Okay," Prince Patrick said. "Warriors let's proceed with caution."

"Sovereign God!" Dylan said, his chin held high. "We proceed in your almighty name!"

"Wait!" Mistress Meredith said, putting up her right hand. "We must dismount."

"Indeed!" Dylan said, nodding his head. "Height is a component." His face screwed up. "I deduce we should crawl."

"Get all the horses into that ravine on the right and both of you lay flat on the ground." Meredith said, dismounting and gesturing towards Godric and Sir Richard. "Don't get up until we say it's clear."

Godric and Sir Richard quickly dismounted and took the reins of all the horses and headed for the ravine.

"Once the horses are in the ravine, Sir Richard and I will lie flat on the ground on the other side of the ravine and hold the reins of the horses." Master Godric said, heading towards the ravine with Sir Richard following quickly behind.

As soon as the horses were in the ravine and Master Godric and Sir Richard were lying down, Dylan got down on his hands and knees. "Everyone descend and imitate me."

Crawling cautiously, they entered the clump of trees. "Everyone lie down on your back." Mistress Meredith said. "There's fiery darts above us."

Master Drew rubbed his chin with his right hand. "Sovereign God, how do we combat that?"

"*Above all, taking the shield of faith, wherewith ye shall be able to quench all the fiery darts of the wicked.*" Dylan said.

"*No weapon that is formed against thee shall prosper.*" Winifred said.

"*And take the helmet of salvation, and the sword of the Spirit, which is the word of God. For the word of God is quick, and powerful, and sharper than any two-edged sword.* Let's use our sword of the Spirit which is a two-edged sword to annihilate the fiery darts." Patrick said.

"Everyone shoot two-edged swords at the place the darts are coming from and proclaim *greater is he that is in you than he that is the world.*" Mistress Meredith said.

"*Greater is he that is in you than he that is in the world!*" They all said in unison, releasing the swords.

Immediately the place lit up like the sun itself, the darts ceased, and all was calm.

"Astounding!" Dylan said, standing to his feet.

"Whew!" Mistress Meredith said, sighing heavily. "I believe the Sovereign God is helping us older folks to be more sensitive to him like Catrin and Griffin. He's enabling us to comprehend the power of his word."

Patrick ran his fingers along the scar from his right temple to his chin. "I sure wish we had known the Sovereign God and the power of his word before."

"It is most exhilarating!" Dylan said, giving a wide grin.

"My whole body is shaking from the power." Master Drew said, grabbing his head with both hands.

"My heart is fluttering with excitement." Gwent said, holding his hands against his chest.

Gwendolyn touched her husband's shoulder. "My heart is fluttering in unison with yours."

"Mine too." Kevyn said, breathing heavily.

Fletcher, Ariana, Falconer, and Heidi all shouted. "*Now thanks be unto God, which always causeth us to triumph in Christ.*"

Archer held his head with both hands. "Wait until I tell Vanora about this."

"Dear me!" Mistress Meredith said, laughing. "I think we'd better let Master Godric and Sir Richard know it's over."

"Great Jehoshaphat!" Rhonda said, shaking both fists. "Is this Déjà vu?"

"Déjà vu undoubtedly." Owen said, gesturing with both hands. "We are observing a Krog generating turmoil with the Humans."

"Oh no!" Matthew said. "With that beast is Arthur, Elton, Hollie, Winter, and Oxford. They are Druxin's worst." He held his chest with both hands, taking a deep breath. "Arthur is third in power under Druxin and Maddock. Those other four are Druxin's Squires." He paused. "We heard all that as they were carrying us to the woods."

As the Pundles caught sight of the Krog, they headed for it. "No!" Catrin said. "They may be stronger than the Krog, but we don't know what kind of evil power those others possess."

Old nodded his head. "Pearl and Pemberton, you both stay in those brushes until I call for you."

Herald Roth patted his Pundle with his left hand. "Okay, Taffy, you stay with Pearl and Pemberton until I call for you."

Griffin rubbed his hands together. "I heard Old say the gold crosses give you supernatural power, but we have no idea if you'll be powerful enough against those five. Once we know what powers you actually have, we can do things differently." He scratched the back of his head with his right hand. "At present, I believe you three should stay behind."

"Griffin's right." Catrin said. "We know the power we possess, but we don't know what they possess. I believe we're more challenging, but I don't want to risk any of you."

"Well, I'm an Elfdin." Herald Roth said, scratching the back of his head with his left hand. "However, what I possess will be made known shortly."

"I was so excited about possessing the power from the Sovereign God that I didn't think about what power Evil Druxin may have in our world." Old's lips vibrated out air. "I believe we'll stay with the Pundles until we understand what power we possess."

Mary nodded her head. "I'm not sure how to use any power from the Sovereign God. I just know how evil the power of Druxin is." She bit her bottom lip. "It seems to me; I should wait until we know what power we possess. I certainly don't want to be left for dead again."

"I must differ with you all." Matthew said. "How can we discover what power we have, if we stay hidden?" He wiped sweat from his forehead with his right hand. "I have this strong impression to go with you all."

"That sounds familiar." Meghan said, twisting her hands. "I've experienced such a feeling when the Sovereign God is urging you to do something you would never do without his prompting."

"Okay." Catrin said. "I believe Matthew is to accompany us."

"*For with God nothing shall be impossible* is what the Sovereign God is telling me." Matthew said, pointing to the gold cross hanging around his neck.

"Warriors!" David said. "Let's proceed."

"Wait!" Griffin said. "We have to go in by twos."

Catrin nodded her head. "Griffin and I are to lead with Owen and Rhonda behind, then David and Meghan with Matthew and Herald Roth behind at the end."

"Lordy me!" Old said, clasping his hands together. "When Matthew quoted the word of the Sovereign God, I knew I was to go."

"Me too." Mary said, touching Old's right arm.

Catrin gestured with her right hand towards Matthew and Herald Roth. "Old and Mary, you two follow them."

Griffin rubbed his hands together. "Warriors, follow me and Catrin."

Mistress Meredith quickly checked on Master Godric and Sir Richard. "Thank the Sovereign God you're both safe."

"The Sovereign God is utilizing the potency of his word." Dylan said, sighing heavily. "We are all astonishment at what transpired."

Godric hung his head. "I've always depended upon his word. Yet, Evil Druxin has made me feel impotent." He rubbed his chin with his right hand. "I know he's from a supernatural world, and I'm from a natural world. But the Bible says, *behold, I give unto you power to tread on serpents and scorpions, and over all the power of the enemy: and nothing shall by any means hurt you.*" His face screwed up. "What am I doing wrong? I seem to have no power over Druxin? Surely, he's the enemy."

Master Drew took Godric's right hand into both his hands. "Let me tell you we are supernatural beings from a supernatural world, but our world spent 400 years using natural warfare."

"I believe," Mistress Meredith interrupted, "fear has you in its hold because Druxin released Maddock from your prison." She closed her eyes and rubbed her forehead with her right hand. "The Sovereign God is saying you'll know what's what shortly. In the meantime, know you've done no wrong." She gestured with her hand. "You're facing an obstacle in your faith and the means to overcome will be made known."

Godric's face screwed up. "I sense him telling me to keep heading for the castle to join the others." His eyes filled with tears. "He just touched me with such love." He wiped his eyes with his right hand. "I've been so concerned about the evil taking over my world, that I've neglected my time with the Sovereign God."

Patrick rubbed the fingers of his right hand along the scar from his right temple to his chin. "I believe if our ancestors hadn't spent so much time fighting Krogs, spent more time worshipping the Sovereign God, we probably wouldn't have fallen into so many years of dark ages."

Master Godric bowed his head. "Sovereign God, thank you for your grace that enables us to continue when we seem so helpless. Your word says *my grace is sufficient for thee: for my strength is made perfect in weakness. Most gladly therefore will I rather glory in my infirmities, that the power of Christ may rest upon me.*"

"Amen!" They all said in unison.

"*For thou, Lord, wilt bless the righteous; with favour wilt thou compass him as with a shield.*" Sir Richard said. "The Lord had given me that verse before I went into battle the first time, and it has comforted me whenever I have faced an enemy. For I knew the Lord was my shield." He placed his right hand on his chest. "I've neglected my time with the Sovereign God and neglected the power of his word. My mind has been looking at the storm of evil trying to destroy my world instead of keeping my eyes on him." He smiled. "I certainly don't want to sink like Peter."

Back at the mountain camp, Dewey Ryn believed his warbands were vigorous warriors prepared to take on Evil Druxin and his evil army. "Well!" Dewey said. "Rowena, my guess is that we're formidable warbands against anything Druxin or Maddock may have in their arsenal of evil."

"My dear husband." Rowena said, hugging him. "I'm boggled at how much supernatural power we possess in this world." She clasped her hands together. "It still addles my mind how the shield of the Sovereign God hid us from that Krog."

Kimball touched his sister's left shoulder. "I know what you mean." He scuffled his right foot on the ground. "It sure would've been great if we'd known the Sovereign God in Oralee during all those years of Druxin and his evil Krogs."

"Yes." Dewey said. "However, we can't think about our ignorance. We must concentrate on never again allowing ourselves to believe evil is more powerful than our Sovereign God. Remember that *greater is he that is in you than he that is in the world.*"

"Amen!" Rowena said. "*If God be for us, who can be against us?*"

Kimball raised both arms and shouted in a loud voice. "*I can do all things through Christ which strengtheneth me!*"

"Now." Dewey said. "We haven't heard from the others, but the Sovereign God is prompting the moment of reckoning has arrived." He stood tall. "Gather all the warbands."

Kimball's face beamed. "Yes, Sir! I think my heart is pounding out of my chest. I'm in a dither." He took a deep breath and exhaled loudly. "The Sovereign God knew how much I wanted to be part of the first warband and has allowed me to be part of this venture."

As Kimball ran to gather the others, Dewey gazed into Rowena's eyes. "I believe we are formidable, but we have no idea how enhanced Druxin's evil powers are in this world. It's obvious ours are incredibly more advanced here. However, we will have to *walk circumspectly, not as fools, but as wise.*" He gestured with both hands. "I believe the Sovereign God wants us to remember to walk cautiously, *lest Satan should get an advantage of us: for we are not ignorant of his devices.*"

Rowena nodded her head. "*But he giveth more grace. Wherefore he saith, God resisteth the proud, but giveth grace unto the humble.* Our power is not to make us arrogant but to humble us that the Sovereign God would bestow us with such ability."

Before Dewey could respond, Kimball and the others were running towards him and Rowena. "We are all here and accounted for." Kimball said, catching his breath. "I do believe excitement has us all in quite a dither."

Dewey motioned with his right hand to calm everyone. "I'm sure Kimball informed you all why I've called this gathering." He pushed his shoulders back, displaying a strong posture, and gestured down the mountain to his right. "We've been training, and I believe the Sovereign God wants us to head towards the direction of that distant forest to the right."

Before he could finish, the warbands began to shout. "*For thou hast girded me with strength unto the battle: thou hast subdued under me those that rose up against me.*"

"*Who is this King of glory? The LORD strong and mighty, the LORD mighty in battle.*" Rowena said, wiping tears from her cheeks.

Dewey observed the five warbands as they stood at attention. "We are formidable warriors, but we must not forget our power comes from the Sovereign God. It is good to be excited, but not thrilled in our supernatural power. Never forget our *help cometh from the Lord, which made heaven and earth.*"

"Amen!" They all said in unison.

"Make sure we have provisions and any essentials needed loaded on the Pundles." Dewey said. "I don't know how long we'll be away from our mountain stronghold or what evil is out there. All I know is the Bible says *have not I commanded thee? Be strong and of a good courage; be not afraid, neither be thou dismayed: for the LORD thy God is with thee whithersoever thou goest.*" He paused. "We are his warriors and he brought us to this world to help the Humans fight the supernatural evil of Druxin." He stepped in front of the first warband. "Warriors! Follow me."

Chapter 7

The Hidden Cavern

MASTER GODRIC SLUMPED IN his saddle. "Thank the Sovereign God!" He gestured towards his left. "Behind that waterfall is the cavern where all the others are safely hidden. The castle is beyond on the left." He paused. "As a matter of fact, if you look closely, you can see the tower that's facing the North."

"I believe I observe it." Dylan said, his face screwing up. "Why are the others within the cavern and not in the castle?"

"We weren't sure what evil powers Druxin and Maddock possessed." Godric rubbed his chin with his right hand. "When Druxin was able to release Maddock from our imprisonment, and whatever he did to Prophet Andrew and Prophetess Deborah, we all felt it necessary to be hidden until we could comprehend what we were dealing with." He gestured with both hands. "That's why we hid our relatives in the old castle so far away. Besides, it was obvious that Druxin and Maddock would be seeking revenge against me and Mistress Edith."

"Godric!" Mistress Edith said, running from the waterfall. "It was my time to watch for your return." She gestured with her right hand towards the waterfall. "Prince Ordway, Princess Ardith Heather, Lady Dawn, Lord Reginald, Lady Catherine, Sir Anthony, Lady Roselee, and I have been taking turns as sentinels." She let out a heavy sigh. "The prophets and prophetesses have been taking care of Andrew and Deborah, doing the cooking, and cleaning."

She clasped her hands together. "They have been incredible since none of our servants are here."

Master Godric dismounted his horse and hugged his wife. "It has been one horrendous journey. Druxin had traps waiting for us." He gestured towards Mistress Meredith and the others. "If the Elfdins hadn't been with Sir Richard and me, we would've been history."

Edith's eyebrows scrunched together. "Master Drew, Mistress Meredith, Prince Patrick, Princess Winifred, Fletcher, Falconer, Archer, Squire Kevyn, Spiritual Mentor Dylan, Gwendolyn, Heidi, and Ariana what are you all doing here? How will you ever get back into Oralee?"

Mistress Meredith smiled. "It seems all the Elfdins of Oralee are now in your world. We believed the Sovereign God wanted us to come and help you defeat Druxin's evil intent to destroy your world." She looked into Mistress Edith's eyes. "We're not concerned about getting back into Oralee. If the Sovereign God hadn't directed us to leave, Druxin's evil would have certainly killed Godric and Richard." She threw up both hands. "Only the Sovereign God knows how many more would've been destroyed by Druxin's traps."

"Praise the Sovereign God for his protection." Mistress Edith's eyebrows scrunched together. "Where are the others?"

Godric clutched his hands together. "The elderly, parents, and children are in the old castle with our relatives and servants, the warriors of the warbands are taking refuge in a mountain in caves, Herald Roth is guarding the entrance into Oralee where Sir Archibald is staying at the request of the Sovereign God." His face screwed up. "And I have no idea what is going on with Griffin, Catrin, David, and Meghan. It seems they were ushered by the Sovereign God to help Owen and Rhonda who were heading into some sort of trouble." He paused. "I'm so pleased prophet Andrew and prophetess Deborah are still living?"

"Yes. They're weakening, but alive." She paused. "Like I said, the other prophets and prophetesses take turns tending to them day and night." Edith gestured towards Meredith. "Druxin has used evil power on them." She shook her head. "We seem to be powerless to combat it. We have no idea what to do."

Mistress Meredith closed her eyes and rubbed her forehead with her right hand. "We must get to them quickly."

As the others dismounted, Godric had them follow him. "As soon as we get into the cavern, Edith will lead you to Andrew and Deborah." He gestured with his right hand. "If you follow me, I'll lead the way. We'll hide our mounts inside one of the smaller caverns with the other horses." He chuckled. "You'll be amazed at the size of this place. It's quite majestic with the smaller caverns and tunnels that lead up to the main cavern. In fact, my grandfather set the huge cavern up like a castle." He paused. "That's why during the last war, our families were safe and comfortable. Those of us who were fighting stayed away from the cavern. We didn't know how the war would go and wanted our families kept safe."

"Wow!" Kevyn said, as they entered behind the waterfall.

Master Godric smiled. "Wait until you actually see the main cavern."

"This is so impressive." Archer said, scratching the back of his head with his right hand. "It's well-designed. Of course nothing compares to the Gold Temple, but this is quite amazing."

"That's the Sovereign God." Fletcher said, gazing up at his surroundings.

"We have Andrew and Deborah in a small alcove off the main cavern." Mistress Edith said. "They require constant care."

Lady Dawn was the first to see them entering the cavern and screamed. "Richard! You're back." She said, running to her husband. "I've been on tenterhooks waiting for your return." She grabbed his face with both hands. "Praise be to the Sovereign God for bringing you back safe and sound."

He gestured towards the Elfdins. "If he hadn't had them come to our world, Master Godric and I would not be here for this reunion. Druxin had traps set for us that we have no power over." He sighed heavily. "It was the Elfdins who handled whatever destruction Druxin had planned for any Humans who came near his evil snares."

"What do you mean?" She gestured towards the Elfdins. "How will you ever get back into Oralee?"

Dylan screwed up his face. "It appears all Elfdins may permanently inhabit your world. The Sovereign God instructed us to depart and succor you in the combat against Druxin and Maddock."

"I believe he's correct." Master Drew said, rubbing his chin with his right hand. "We obeyed the Sovereign God and now we're in his hands."

Winifred nodded her head. "It seems we've come here to understand the power of his word."

"We quoted that *we can do all things through Christ.*" Patrick said, rubbing his right temple with his right hand. "But until we entered this world, we didn't really comprehend the incredible power of his word to combat evil."

"Wow!" Falconer said. "This place is enormous."

Edith interrupted. "Mistress Meredith!" She said, pointing to her right. "Andrew and Deborah are ahead in that small alcove to the right."

"Drew and Dylan, please come with me." Meredith said.

"This looks bad." Master Drew said, rubbing his chin with his right hand.

Meredith gazed at Andrew and Deborah. "They appear to be dead, but I see life in their eyes." Her eyebrows squished together. "Let me seek the Sovereign God, for I have no idea what this is." She closed her eyes and rubbed her forehead with her right hand. "The word is our instruction manual that says, *they shall lay hands on the sick, and they shall recover.*"

"Amen!" Dylan said. "*By whose stripes ye were healed.*"

"*For I am the Lord that healeth thee.*" Drew said.

"Okay." Meredith said, getting down on her knees at their heads. "Apparently it's no different than any other malady." She gazed at Drew and Dylan. "Let's lay a hand on both of them and pray." She said, laying a hand on each head.

Drew and Dylan kneeled at their feet and placed a hand on each leg. "We're ready." Dylan said.

Meredith bowed her head. "Sovereign God, we bind the powers of Hell that have come against your prophets and loose the power of Heaven." She stood up. "Andrew and Deborah, rise and be healed in the name of the Sovereign God!"

Immediately the young prophets trembled, sat up, and stood to their feet. "They need to eat something." Meredith said.

Edith, who had been watching, nodded her head. "Follow me to the cavern where the meals are prepared." She gestured with both hands. "I don't understand why we couldn't do that. We know the power of the word." She paused. "I know you're from a supernatural world, but shouldn't the power of the word be the same here?"

Meredith's face screwed up. "That's a good question." She paused. "There must be an answer to it. I know we're supernatural beings and possess more supernatural power than you Humans, but the power of the word should have no bearing on your ability. The word is supernatural in its ability."

"Excuse me." Andrew said. "Who are you little people? Where did you come from? You look like the one who paralyzed us." He scratched the back of his head with his right hand. "All I know is that everyone here has prayed and prayed over us." He shrugged his shoulders. "To be honest, I was beginning to think the Sovereign God was taking me home." He gave out a heavy sigh. "It was most difficult, because I was convinced he had some plan for me in ministering." He paused. "I kept hearing, *by whose stripes ye were healed*, but no matter how many times it ran through my mind, I couldn't move."

"I question if their situation is different owing to Evil Druxin being a supernatural being." Dylan said, his face screwing up. "After all, they are natural beings." He gestured with his left hand. "However, the word says, *and these signs shall follow them that believe; In my name they shall lay hands on the sick, and they shall recover.*"

Meredith nodded her head. "That would make sense." She turned towards Mistress Edith. "You're all believers in the Sovereign God. Laying your hands on them should have healed them."

"This is all so strange to us." Edith said, sighing heavily. "We prophets and prophetesses have always been the ones with the power in our world." She gestured with both hands. "Now, Druxin has us appearing powerless by releasing Maddock from our prison like it was nothing." She touched Meredith's shoulder with her right hand. "We even fasted before praying. What are we doing wrong?"

"All I know is that when Godric asked that, the Sovereign God said fear had him in its hold, but he'd done no wrong." Meredith said, looking directly into Edith's eyes. "Apparently something is missing, and you'll know what it is shortly."

Arthur along with his sergeants Elton, Hollie, Winter, and Oxford were walking behind Soot as people ran frantically away. "I can't wait to see the look on my father's face when I hurl a few bolts by him." Arthur said, giving a guttural chortle. "None of you must do anything to him. I intend to torture him until his last breath like my mother suffered."

Hollie, biting a hangnail on her right thumb, watched as Soot was clawing at people as they tried to run away. When a little lad fell down, Soot headed straight for him. Hollie screamed. "No!" She ran to the lad, picked him up, and held him close.

Suddenly a ball of fire landed in front of Soot, stopping her from proceeding. "You'll not touch that little lad." Herald said, standing firm.

Arthur sent a bolt at Hollie, that fizzled before it reached her. "What was that?" He said, his face screwing up.

"It's described as the supernatural power of the Sovereign God." Rhonda said, shooting her left fist into the air. "All your power is second-hand power from the devil who is a created be-ing. Original power is from the Sovereign God who is the Creator of all powers."

At that, Arthur sent a ball of fire towards Rhonda. "Take that, you little wench."

"Don't believe she will." Owen said, releasing a ball of fire that consumed Arthur's.

"Squires!" Arthur said. "Take out Hollie and then take out those three."

"I believe you better think twice about that order." Catrin said, punching the air with her right fist. "It seems you may have taken on more than you're capable of."

Griffin rubbed his hands together. "I must agree with Catrin."

"It does seem that way." David said, rubbing the back of his neck with his right hand.

Meghan nodded her head. "I must agree with the others."

"It seems you botched this one up, young Human." Herald said, looking directly into Arthur's eyes.

"Lordy me!" Old said, clasping his hands together. "Young apprentice, I don't believe you know the power of these Elfdins."

"I believe we are examples of such power." Matthew said, gesturing with his right hand towards Mary. "He reached into his tunic and pulled out his cross. "This gives us supernatural power from the Sovereign God."

"We left you both for dead." Arthur said, grabbing his head with both hands. "Druxin said you would be food for the vultures."

"Well, you have two choices." Griffin said, making a tent with his fingers and tapping his lips with his forefingers. "You can leave here now, or we'll be forced to destroy you."

Elton's eyes bulged. "Arthur, perhaps we need to get back to Druxin and Maddock and let them know these little people are here."

"Yes." Winter and Oxford said in unison.

Arthur gave a guttural chortle. "I'm sure Druxin will know how to take care of these." He gestured with his right hand. "Soot, follow us out of here."

As Arthur, Elton, Winter, Oxford, and Soot all left, Chester headed towards Matthew, glared into his lad's eyes, and gave him a hug. "My lad, I have sorely missed you."

"Father, please forgive my rebellion." Matthew said, tears rolling down his cheeks.

Hollie watched Matthew and his father, held the little lad tight, and sobbed loudly. "Grandma, I'm so sorry for thinking I could be part of the knights of vile power."

Catrin placed her right hand on Hollie's left shoulder. "Are you okay?"

Hollie gazed into Catrin's eyes. "You're the size of Druxin, but you're not evil." She looked down at the ground. "My grandmother died, and I became angry at the Sovereign God." She looked up. "She was all the family I had left." She bit her bottom lip. "Will the Sovereign God forgive me?"

"Lordy me!" Old said, reaching into his pocket to pull out a gold cross. "The Sovereign God forgives all repented sins." He placed a gold cross around her neck.

As soon as the cross touched Hollie's chest, she fell prostrate on the ground. "Oh grandma, I know you're with him." She sat up. "I'm forgiven, and I'll honor my grandmother's memory by living for the Sovereign God as she did."

"Wait a minute!" Chester said. "Archibald, what are you doing here and who are these little people clothed alike in forest green?"

"They came to help us fight the evil trying to destroy our world." Old pointed towards Rhonda. "Her horse lost its shoe, and we need you to fix it."

"That's something I can surely do."

"Father!" Matthew said, wiping sweat from his forehead with his right hand. "I'm to accompany them to war against Druxin and Maddock. I'm now part of the Sovereign God's army to combat evil."

"I'll not stop you from doing his will." Chester said, hugging his lad. "May he keep you safe."

"He now possesses the power of the cross of the Sovereign God." Herald said, gesturing with his right hand towards Old. "As a matter of fact, he'll give all you who believe in the Sovereign God a cross."

Griffin made a tent with his forefingers and patted his lips. "I believe it would be wise if everyone left the town. Is there any place to hide unknown to the one who led those Humans earlier?"

"That was Arthur." Matthew said. "His father is the vicar here."

"It's strange you should ask that." Chester said. "My grandfather told me many times about a hidden cavern his grandfather told him about." He scratched the back of his head with his right hand. "All he knew is that it was accessible through stone stairs." He paused. "After Matthew left, I went to the ruins of the old castle in the woods. It used to belong to my great-great-grandfather before it was ruined during a war." He sighed heavily. "Anyway, I was seeking the Sovereign God to protect my lad. As I kneeled at one of the southern walls, I noticed something odd." He grabbed his face with both hands. "The closer I examined it, I realized it seemed to push in. I pushed hard and almost fell down the stairs." He gestured with both hands. "At the bottom was the entrance to a huge cavern that must have been used to protect the castle inhabitants during the war." He gave a wide grin. "It's in excellent condition with separate places apparently made special for the family and relatives."

"Is there any way Arthur can know about it?" Griffin said, gesturing with his right hand.

"No! As a matter of fact, I haven't told anyone before today." Chester said. "Truth be told, I've been wondering why I found it." He gestured with both hands. "It's my property, but I've never done much with it."

David folded his arms and shook his head. "It was definitely the Sovereign God who led you to the cavern." He rubbed his hands together. "I believe you should get those who will follow you into it quickly."

"That should be the whole town. Arthur has been the only evil one in the town." He paused and looked down. "That's why it was so heartbreaking when Matthew left." He placed his left hand on his lad's right shoulder. "But I knew he was struggling with something, and the Sovereign God would help him through it."

"Bring supplies, weapons, and whatever essentials needed." Catrin said, twirling her raven black hair around her right forefinger.

Meghan shuffled her feet and looked down. "I believe we have to leave here quickly."

Owen gestured with his left hand. "I perceive Arthur will return with Druxin."

Old pulled a handful of gold crosses out of his saddle bag. "Chester, take one of these. You need to give one to Arthur's father, and others who serve the Sovereign God." He clasped his hands together. "I don't believe you will have to fight Druxin, but you'll possess power to sense evil and combat it." He placed his right hand on Chester's left shoulder. "Make sure some of you can hunt for food if necessary." Old held up a cross. "These crosses give us Humans supernatural power from the Sovereign God."

Chester shoed Rhonda's horse, saddled horses for Herald, Matthew, Hollie, and Mary. They gave their farewells, and set out to meet up with the others.

Chapter 8

Faith Or Fear

DRUXIN'S EYES GLARED, HIS nostrils flared, and he shot bolts of lightning into the air. "What do you mean, you were beaten? You're the most powerful Human in this world next to Maddock." He grabbed Arthur's left arm with his right hand. "Who are they who have supposedly beaten you?"

Arthur hung his head. "All I heard was Elfdins and Catrin."

"Catrin!" Druxin said, shaking Arthur until he fell to his knees. "Who told you they were Elfdins?"

"Some old man said he didn't believe I knew the power of these Elfdins." He paused. "When I saw Matthew and Ivey completely healed and ready to fight with them, it baffled me. I just thought if we got back to you, we would get instructions to defeat them."

"How many of these Elfdins were there?"

"There were three young females, three young males, and an older male." He clenched his teeth. "It was the old Elfdin who shot a ball of fire to stop Soot and told me I really botched it up."

"Let me see which Elfdins are actually here." Druxin said, touching Soot's head with both hands, and shutting his eyes. "It appears we have Griffin and Catrin the two in line to be the Great Prophet and Great Prophetess. Then there's Owen and Rhonda in line to be the Spiritual Mentors, along with David and Meghan who are in line to be Prince and Princess of the Elfdins." He snickered. "What in Oralee is Herald Roth doing with them?" He cupped his hands together. "Outside of Herald, they have sent the heirs who are their most formidable warriors." He gave a wide grin. "We shall destroy them once and for all."

"What are the Elfdins doing in this world? If they're here, they have no way of getting back to Oralee." Maddock said, sneering. "What fools." He brushed his long gray hair back with his hands. "I believe the old man must be Sir Archibald Godwin, which means he must have requested their help."

"Now, the question is where are the rest of the Humans who visit Oralee." Druxin said, gesturing towards Arthur. "You are sure there were only three Humans with the Elfdins?"

"Yes." Arthur gave a heavy sigh. "I knew you would be able to defeat them." He gave a guttural chortle. "There's no one more powerful than you." He gestured with his right hand. "One of those Elfdins said my power was second-hand power from the devil and hers was the original power from the Sovereign God who created all powers."

Druxin's eyebrows squished together. "Where's the thin blond Squire? Was she destroyed in the battle?"

"She saved a little lad before Soot could get to him." Elton said. "When Arthur tried to take her out, an Elfdin girl with ash blond hair destroyed his bolt."

"Rhonda!" Druxin said, eyes glaring.

Winter interrupted. "Then when Arthur tried to take the first Elfdin girl out, an Elfdin boy with the same color hair stopped his ball of fire."

"Owen!" Druxin said, shooting a bolt into the air.

Oxford shook his head. "Arthur no sooner ordered us to take out Hollie and the two young ones and the old Elfdin when more Elfdins appeared."

"It was that Catrin who said I had taken on more than I can handle." Arthur said, his voice quaking. "It was the Elfdin male with black hair like yours that told me we had two choices. We could leave or be destroyed."

"Griffin!" Druxin said, nodding his head.

Arthur shrugged his shoulders. "When I saw Matthew and Ivey standing there completely healed, I just believed it was wiser to get back to you."

"Never let fear rule you. You are invincible." Druxin said, eyes glaring. "Do you hear me?"

"Yes, sir." Arthur said, looking down.

"I'm not surprised at Matthew and Ivey being healed." Druxin said, fingering his black beard. "Possessing incredible healing abilities is part of our birthright." Druxin said, cupping his hands. "However, I'm the most powerful of all Elfdins."

"You mean you're one of them?" Arthur said, eyes bulging.

"I'm an Elfdin, but I am not one of them." Druxin said, cupping his hands. "They serve the Sovereign God who has gotten in my way too many times." He made a wide grin. "With the Elfdins being confined to this world, I will destroy them and him once and for all. No power can defeat me." He gestured with his right hand towards a large oak tree. "Be plucked up by the roots and be thrown into that distant lake." Immediately the tree uprooted and landed into the lake.

Maddock, Arthur, Elton, Winter, and Oxford all shouted in unison. "Grand Master Druxin!"

Druxin fingered his black beard with his right hand. "I do believe it's time to gather all our apprentices with Arthur, Elton, Winter, and Oxford each commanding 1,000. Maddock will take command of the 5,000 graduates, and I will follow with the Krogs." Druxin said, eyes glaring. "We're the knights of vile power and have a most formidable army to overtake these Elfdins." He snickered. "Along with Carbon, Nightshade, and Soot, we'll put an end to their interference and destroy the Sovereign God at the same time." He cupped his hands. "Our army will commence first thing in the morning."

Mistress Meredith closed her eyes and rubbed her forehead with her right hand. "I strongly sense that only a few Humans are to accompany us as the Crusade commences to meet up with Griffin,

Catrin, and the others." Her face screwed up. "I mean no offense, but I believe we won't require everyone's help. It appears the Sovereign God wants you to use the time to hunt for food and preserve it. Druxin left many without food." She gestured with her right hand. "I believe he is directing Master Godric, Mistress Edith, Prophet Andrew, and Prophetess Deborah to accompany us." She paused. "All others are to remain behind in the cavern."

Sir Richard nodded his head. "I thought I would be accompanying the Crusade, but I have this strong impression to stay here and lead the hunting." He smiled. "That's one thing I'm proficient at."

Dylan gestured with his left hand. "It is astounding at the vitality of Andrew and Deborah after their affliction. Indubitably, the Sovereign God has designs for them."

"He just impressed me with these words, *in God I will praise his word, in God I have put my trust; I will not fear what flesh can do unto me.*" Andrew said, his face screwing up. "I've never been told that before." He gestured with both hands. "I believe we're being told to trust in his word and faith doesn't fear anything."

Godric rubbed his chin with his right hand. "I realize we've been fearful of Druxin since he liberated Maddock out of my prison." He sighed, heavily. "It's most unsettling to be so confused about what I'm capable of. My foundation seems to be shaking."

Prince Patrick ran his fingers along the scar from his right temple to his chin. "You Humans have been serving the Sovereign God for years. Even while we went through our 400 years of dark age, you followed him." He gazed at Master Godric. "It was you Humans that directed us to the Bible to learn about the Sovereign God."

"It's his word that's taken us through the snares of Druxin. The power of the word demolished all the fiery darts and obstacles." Master Drew said, gesturing with both hands. "We are to trust his word and fear nothing. The Bible says, *the Lord is on my side; I will not fear: what can man do unto me?* All supernatural power comes from the power of his word."

Mistress Meredith interrupted. "The bible says, *for God has not given us a spirit of fear, but of power and of love and of a sound mind.*" She gestured towards Godric with her right hand. "I believe fear has caused you to forget the power of his word."

"Perhaps that's why you aren't able to overcome Druxin's evil." Archer said, scratching the back of head with his right hand. "Fear restrains us."

Dylan nodded his head. "I concur."

Mistress Meredith closed her eyes and rubbed her forehead with her right hand. "Without faith in the power of the word, there is fear which generates doubt. We either walk in faith or fear. There's no middle ground." She paused. "Because we believe in the power of the word, it has been a two-edged sword for us." She gestured with her right hand. "If you Humans have forgotten the power of the word like we forgot the Sovereign God, you have allowed fear to overcome your faith." She looked into Godric's eyes. "Fear has made you powerless against the supernatural evil trying to take over this world."

Godric nodded his head. "I believe you're right. When I discovered Druxin had released Maddock, I felt fear, and I began to doubt what I could do." His face screwed up. "To be honest, I still don't understand how he did it. I believe it has rattled me more than I know."

Gwent interrupted. "I believe we need to head out and find out about Rhonda, Owen, and those who went to help them."

"I know they're quite challenging warriors, but I believe we should be with them." Archer said.

Winifred nodded her head. "I must admit about being concerned about my bairns. I know they're sensitive to the Sovereign God, but I would be more comfortable finding them."

"I acquiesce." Dylan said, sighing heavily. "Owen is exceedingly formidable. However, I desire to locate my lad."

"Okay, warriors." Patrick said. "Let the Crusade commence with caution."

Meredith put up her right hand. "I believe we'll keep the same formation with Dylan, Drew, and I in front, followed by Patrick

and Winifred with Archer and Kevyn following. The rest will follow as before with Godric, Edith, Andrew, and Deborah behind."
She gazed at Godric and Edith. "I mean no offense, but we have
been tested against Druxin's evil. I believe wisdom would have you
stay behind until you understand why fear seems to have a hold
of you both since Druxin released Maddock out of your supernatural prison." She paused. "You must trust in the Sovereign God.
Remember, he made clear you've done no wrong. Yet, fear has
overtaken your faith and caused you to believe there's something
wrong with you. Anyway, all should be known shortly."

Godric rubbed his chin with his right hand. "I take no offense. If Sir Richard and I had been in the lead before, we would
be dead." His face screwed up. "All I know is the Sovereign God is
trying to show me something that I have yet to grasp."

Edith placed her hands on her hips. "I'm in agreement with
my husband. Maddock being released from our prison has rattled
me. I believe fear has me in doubt of what I'm capable of." Her
eyebrows scrunched together. "Although the Bible says, *behold, I
give unto you power to tread on serpents and scorpions, and over all
the power of the enemy: and nothing shall by any means hurt you*,
I find myself wavering and fearing Druxin's power. I'm like a reed
tossed." She gestured towards Godric with her right hand. "Yet, I
sense we'll overcome all this by joining in the Crusade. I believe
we must face this giant like David and trust the Sovereign God."

Chapter 9

The Armies Assemble

GRIFFIN STARED TO HIS left. "Catrin, I believe I see Dewey Ryn with the warbands heading in our direction."

"Yes!" Catrin said, punching the air with her right fist. "I see the Pundles." She watched as they marched closer.

"Wow!" Matthew said, gazing at the warbands. "I didn't know there were so many of you Elfdins."

"There has to be 30,000 at least in those warbands." Griffin said, rubbing his hands together.

"I believe Druxin is in for a rude awakening when he sees the size of that army." Mary said, her eyes widening.

Hollie looked down at the ground. "Will the Sovereign God allow me to fight with you after what I did?"

"Lordy me!" Old said, clasping his hands together. "If he hadn't accepted you, the cross wouldn't have done what it did when I placed it around your neck."

"He is truly forgiving when we repent." David said, rubbing the back of head with his right hand. "We Elfdins forgot about him for 400 years through Druxin's deception."

"Indubitably compassionate!" Rhonda said, fidgeting with her left earlobe.

"Categorically!" Owen said, combing his ash blond hair back with the fingers of his left hand.

"*But he giveth more grace. Wherefore he saith, God resisteth the proud, but giveth grace unto the humble.*" Matthew said, touching the gold cross hanging from his neck. "Thank the Sovereign God for his grace."

Hollie hugged the cross with both hands against her chest. "I don't know what is ahead, but I'm forgiven. My life belongs to the Sovereign God."

"Well, I'm quite boggled." Dewey Ryn said, grabbing his head with both hands. "Catrin, David, Griffin, Meghan, Owen, and Rhonda, what in Oralee are you doing here? Where are the others?"

"It's a long story." Catrin said, twirling her raven black hair around her right forefinger. "However, I must admit, we're quite pleased to see all of you."

Griffin nodded his head. "We've encountered some of Druxin's snares along our journey, and we believe he'll be heading our way towards a town we recently left."

"Some of Druxin's Human apprentices tried to destroy the town." Meghan said, twisting her hands together. "Apparently, one of them is the lad of the Vicar in the town."

"His name is Arthur, and he hates his father for letting his mother die." Matthew said.

"Excuse me." Rowena interrupted. "We know Old, but who are the other three Humans? I've never seen them in Oralee."

"It appears we were apprentices of Maddock, until the Sovereign God opened our eyes." Matthew said, touching the gold cross hanging from his neck.

"That's right." Old said, gesturing towards Matthew. "This is my cousin's lad, and he's now a lad of the Sovereign God."

"Wait a minute!" Dewey said, glaring at Herald Roth. "I thought you were supposed to be guarding the entrance into Oralee?"

"It was negated." Rhonda said.

Herald nodded his head. "Once the Sovereign God instructed Old to leave, there was no need to guard the entrance." He shrugged his shoulders. "There's no one left to guard."

"Excuse me." David said, rubbing the back of his neck with his right hand. "It's getting late. I believe we should all set up some sort of camp in those woods to our right. We'll take turns standing guard."

"Druxin won't be travelling at night. He'll set out at sunrise." Griffin said, making a tent with his fingers and tapping his lips with his forefingers. "We'll let the Pundles stand guard while we get a good night's sleep. Whatever Druxin has planned, we must be alert."

David nodded his head. "I believe you're right. We could all use some rest."

"Lordy me!" Old said. "I feel like I've been in battle with all that's been happening." He threw his head back, let out a peal of laughter, and grabbed the gold cross hanging from his neck. "Yet, I feel like Caleb ready to take on the Canaanites with the power of the Sovereign God's cross flowing though me."

Dewey Ryn's eyebrows squished together. "Where did you get that gold cross?"

Old looked down at his cross. "I found them in Oralee along with some old parchments. It was revealed that this little gold cross gives Humans supernatural power like the Elfdins in our world." He clasped his hands together. "Plus, when all the Elfdins are together, I have great news for them."

Druxin and his evil army were ready to move out at sunrise. "I want each of you to comprehend there isn't an Elfdin or Human more powerful than me." He glared at Arthur. "Do you think you can understand that truth?"

"Yes, sir." Arthur said. "I never doubted your power. When Matthew and Ivey stood there with them, I wasn't sure of what power I possessed."

"When Rhonda stopped your bolt, did you send another?"

"I sent a ball of fire at her." Arthur said, looking down. "However, it was stopped by the other Elfdin."

Druxin fingered his black beard. "So, you let Owen get away with that." His eyes glared. "You allowed them to frighten you." He nostrils flared. "You're the third most powerful being in this world." He pointed with his right forefinger. "You are Knight Arthur, and you are invincible."

"I've been made a fool." Arthur said, clenching his teeth. "That won't happen a second time." His nostrils enlarged. "I can assure you I will destroy those Elfdins."

"That's more like it." Druxin said, snickering. "We're an unbeatable army who'll defeat the Sovereign God and all his followers once and for all and rule this world with all others as our servants."

"This is so exhilarating." Maddock said. "I still can't get over what a marvelous day it was when I met you." He sneered. "I really would like to keep Master Godric and Mistress Edith alive to be my servants. Their death would end their misery, but living the rest of their life as my servants would be so satisfying."

Druxin gave a wide grin. "I do believe you're becoming more cunning by the day. It never occurred to me how rewarding it would be to make Catrin my slave wife with Griffin, Owen, and Rhonda as servants." He cupped his hands together. "Listen up! Master Godric, Mistress Edith, Catrin, Griffin, Owen, and Rhonda are to be immobilized, but not killed." His eyes glared. "Do I make myself clear? If one of you disobeys my order, you'll be instantly killed."

Arthur's emerald eyes beamed. "Would I be allowed to keep Ivey as my slave wife? She is quite a beauty. I know she despises me, and that's what makes it more intriguing."

"My lad, you're truly making me proud I chose you." Druxin said, giving a loud chortle. "It'll be my pleasure to give her to you." He gestured with his right hand. "The same instructions go for Ivey. If she is harmed, it will be instant death for the offender."

"Well, seeing we're getting slave wives." Maddock said, sneering. "I believe I would have Princess Ardith Heather as mine." He rubbed his hands together. "I've always admired her beauty, but never thought of actually having her as my wife." He shrugged his shoulders. "I believe she's the most beautiful woman I've ever seen."

Druxin nodded his head. "Let it be so."

"Okay." Maddock said, rubbing his hands together. "I believe our army is ready to move out."

"Now, I want you all to remember, you do nothing until I give the command." Druxin said, his eyes glaring. "A false move could be disastrous. They're supernatural beings capable of supernatural powers. If they can fool you into believing they're more powerful, you'll let down your guard." He gestured towards Arthur and his sergeants. "As Arthur, Elton, Winter, and Oxford experienced with their Elfdin encounter."

"We know who is more powerful." Arthur said. "They'll not fool us again with their false display of power and bogus words of destroying us."

"Remember." Maddock said. "Cowering is not what this army does. We're the most powerful force in this world. We're the knights of vile power."

"Let's destroy the intruders and those with them." Druxin said, eyes glaring. "This is our world to dominate."

"Grand Master Druxin!" They all said, raising their fists. "We're yours to command."

Griffin just laid down when a Pundle nudged him. "What is it?" He said, jumping to his feet, and seeing figures in the distant heading towards them. "Everyone to your feet. We have company."

"Oh my!" Catrin said, gazing towards the company heading their way. "I believe it's Master Godric with the others."

"Incredible!" Owen said, kicking the ground with his left foot.

"Yes, it is." Dewey said, shaking his head. "I see Prince Patrick and Princes Winifred."

They waited until the others were inside the camp. "We're glad you're here. It seems Druxin is about to wage war on us tomorrow." Catrin said, twirling her raven black hair around her right forefinger.

"What are you doing here?" Mistress Meredith said, gesturing towards Old.

"Lordy me! I have so much to tell you all." He said, throwing back his head and letting out a peal of laughter.

"Indubitably!" Rhonda said, doing a two-step. "It is most incredible."

"Wait a minute!" Dylan said. "Did I hear Druxin is about to attack?"

"Yes." Griffin said. "Catrin, Rhonda, Owen, David, Meghan, Herald, Old, and some of his previous followers had a confrontation with some of his apprentices who tried to destroy a town."

"It was Arthur, the son of the town Vicar." Old said, nodding his head. "He was out to kill all the inhabitants of the town." He clasped his hands together. "However, when Rhonda, Griffin, Owen, Catrin, David, Meghan, and Herald confronted him, he and the others left."

"Okay." Mistress Meredith said, her eyebrows squishing together. "But what is the incredible news you have to tell us?"

"I believe we've all been waiting for you to tell us." Meghan said, twisting her hands together.

"Perhaps, this would be the time, or we'll never get any sleep." David said, rubbing the back of his neck with his right hand.

"Let's have those who traveled with Master Godric on the way to the hidden cavern sit over on that little hill." Mistress Meredith said, pointing to her right. "Then we can pass it along to the others."

"I believe Dewey, Rowena, and Kimball should join us." Patrick said, rubbing his temple with his right hand.

"Yes. I agree." Catrin said. "He's been telling us some incredible things the Sovereign God has taught him."

"It was Phenomenal!" Owen said.

"They believed the word saying, *but thou, O Lord, art a shield for me*, and a Krog didn't see them." David said, clasping his hands together.

"It was like they were invisible hiding behind the shield of the Sovereign God." Herald said, patting Taffy's head.

"Wow!" Kevyn said, his brown eyes bulging.

"It seems you Elfdins are empowered with more supernatural power than you even realized." Godric said, rubbing his chin with his right hand.

"Lordy me!" Old said, laughing. "You're all going to be overwhelmed with my news."

"Let's get everyone situated." Mistress Meredith said, looking into Old's eyes. "I believe it's imperative we hear what you have to say."

"Let's assemble on that hill like my Ma suggested." Griffin said, pointing to his left. "That way we can also keep watch on the camp."

"Do Deborah and I come too?" Andrew asked, his face screwing up.

"Lordy me!" Old said, clasping his hands. "It involves all Humans and Elfdins."

"Do I fetch your saddle bag?" Matthew said.

"That's part of the news." Old said, throwing back his head and letting out a peal of laughter. "Without that, I can't distribute the gold crosses."

"This is most exciting." Meghan said, sitting down.

Old motioned for all to be quiet. "I believe I should address the Elfdins first." He said, his lips vibrating as he blew out air. "When I was left in Oralee, the Sovereign God showed me a hidden door in one of the Human figurines. Inside were gold crosses on gold chains that I will explain shortly." He paused. "Anyway, there were parchments explaining everything." He clasped his hands together. "You Elfdins don't need a gold cross to get back into Oralee."

"Praise the Sovereign God!" Falconer said.

"Amen to that!" Master Drew said, grabbing his head with both hands.

"That's such heartwarming news." Winifred said, her face beaming.

"Lordy me! There's more." Old said, gesturing for them to be still. "Now that all the Elfdins have left Oralee, there's no more time difference between the two worlds." He reached into his saddle bag and took out some gold crosses. "The most exciting part is these gold crosses give us Humans supernatural powers in our world like the Elfdins." He shrugged his shoulders. "Of course, the Elfdins are supernatural beings and will always have more power than us."

He threw back his head and let out a peal of laughter. "However, as soon as I put my cross on, I felt a surge of power. I actually feel younger. I feel like Caleb ready to combat the Canaanites." He handed a cross to Master Godric, Mistress Edith, Prophet Andrew, and Prophetess Deborah. "Put these on."

"This must be what the Sovereign God meant when he said there was a missing component, and we would know what it was shortly." Mistress Edith said, putting on her cross.

"Exactly!" Master Godric said, putting on his cross.

"What just happened?" Mistress Edith said, falling backwards. "*For God hath not given us the spirit of fear; but of power.*" Edith said, getting up.

"I believe it would be more powerful for you and Godric because of your positions." Griffin said, scratching the back of his head with his right hand.

"It must be so." Godric said, getting up. "*The Lord is the strength of my life: of whom shall I be afraid?*" He said, clutching his hands together. "We allowed doubt to fill us with fear. We are to *be strong in the Lord, and in the power of his might.*" He paused. "I sense a power unlike anything I've known before."

"Whew!" Deborah said, I've never felt such elation. "It's truly *joy unspeakable and full of glory.*"

"*The Lord thy God in the midst of thee is mighty; he will save, he will rejoice over thee with joy.*" Andrew said, tears streaming down his cheeks. "The Sovereign God has endowed us with supernatural power to overcome evil."

"Lordy me!" Old said. "It gave me such joy seeing you prophets receive his supernatural power." He clasped his hands together. "I guess it's the same for Humans as it is for Elfdins. The higher the calling, the more supernatural power is given to enable the person to fulfill the calling."

"*If any man minister, let him do it according to the ability which God giveth, that God in all things may be glorified.*" Griffin said, scratching the back of his head with his right hand. "We have always known that truth because of our status according to our height. However, since we've known the Sovereign God, we understand our various gifts and talents were given for us to fulfill the ministry he has given us."

"I sense the Sovereign God wants us to be in the town before Druxin and his evil army get there." Catrin said, twirling her raven black hair around her right forefinger. "They have no idea the town is abandoned of its inhabitants. So, we'll have to be there before sunrise."

"Yes!" Griffin said, nodding his head. "Druxin will set out at sunrise."

"Wait a minute!" Catrin said, her eyebrows scrunching together. "I sense the Pundles should be kept separate. We have no idea what Druxin and his evil army are capable of. The Pundles are physically more powerful than Krogs, but they can't battle evil powers."

"Indubitably!" Rhonda said. "We must shelter the Pundles."

"I certainly wouldn't want to lose Pearl and Pemberton." Old said, shaking his head. "Is there some place to keep them?"

"I believe they could stay at the ruins outside the town." Matthew said, his eyebrows scrunching together. "All the townspeople are hidden in the cavern beneath."

"That's an excellent idea." Griffin said. "I believe Dewey should set up the warbands in front of the Pundles with Kimball in charge. Then he, Rowena, and the first warband will be situated inside the town. The rest of us will be waiting at the entrance of the town."

"Well, let's get some rest." Dewey said, standing up. "I'll inform those leading the various warbands of what has transpired and let them handle passing the information along."

"All I know is I'm worn out." Meghan said, twisting her hands.

"Affirmative." Owen said, combing his ash blond hair back with his fingers.

"I'm just boggled that we can go back to Oralee." Fletcher said.

"Undeniably!" Dylan said.

Winifred's faced beamed. "The Sovereign God is a mazer."

"I'm sure this is a nice world to visit, but I'm looking forward to going back to Oralee." Prince Patrick said, running his fingers along the scar from his right temple to his chin.

"All I know is we must be ready to meet whatever evil Druxin and Maddock are planning tomorrow." Godric said, grinning. "Besides, I feel like something in me is ready to burst forth."

"I feel it too." Andrew said, grabbing his head with both hands.

"Well, I believe we'll have to keep it under until tomorrow. We need to rest." Mistress Edith said, grinning.

"Affirmative." Dylan said. "We must be recuperated to contend against the malevolent powers of Druxin."

"May the Sovereign God protect us all." Drew said, rubbing his chin with his right hand.

Patrick ran his fingers along the scar from his right temple to his chin. "All I know is that when I received this scar, I didn't know the power of the Sovereign God's word. Now, we go forth in his power not in ours."

"What he's shown us during our time in this world is that his supernatural word will quench all the fiery darts of evil." Mistress Meredith said.

"Great Jehoshaphat!" Owen said, shooting his left fist up in the air. "It's been astonishing."

Chapter 10

War Of Good Versus Evil

Finally, I'll have my revenge on the Sovereign God and his followers." Grand Master Druxin said, thrusting his chest out. "They think they had the victory over me the last time, but this isn't Oralee. In this world, I am supreme." He patted Carbon on the head. "Well, my lad, this day has been long in coming." He made a wide grin. "I'll destroy the Elfdins, the Humans, and the Sovereign God at the same time."

"Arthur wants to be the first one to enter the town." Maddock said, hurrying to Druxin. "He wants revenge on his Vicar father."

"Vicar?" Druxin said. "I didn't know his father was a Vicar." He fingered his black beard with his right hand. "I believe the lad is more encouraging by the day."

"I think it was a lucky day when I discovered him." Maddock said, brushing his long gray hair back with his hands. "Well, I'd better get back to my command." He laughed. "Everyone is in high spirits. Our adversaries are in for quite a surprise when they see the knights of vile power coming toward them. This army is indestructible."

"We'll prove once and for all that evil is more powerful than good." Druxin said, his lip curling. "I've waited over 400 years for this day." His eyes glared. "That's why everyone must wait for my command. I know how the Elfdins work, and I'll defeat them and their Sovereign God." He cupped his hands. "Now, get back to your command. Tell Arthur he has my permission to be first in the town after I give the command to proceed." He gestured with his right hand. "Make sure the Squires adhere to my orders."

Dewey Ryn set up the warbands at the ruins to protect the area where the townspeople were hiding in the cavern, while Griffin, Catrin, and the rest made ready at the entrance of the town. "I doubt any will get this far." Dewey said, gesturing towards the castle ruins. "Griffin said I'm to get you all in place with Kimball in charge. Then I and Rowena will take the first warband inside the town." He paused. "It's essential that none get past us."

"If they do, we'll see they get no further." Kimball said, matter-of-factly.

"Okay!" Dewey said, gesturing with his right hand. "Rowena and the first warband follow me."

Rowena touched his right arm. "Shouldn't we ask the Sovereign God to be a shield to protect the Pundles?"

"Of course." Dewey said, nodding his head. "They have no supernatural powers we know of. They've been so loyal to us even before we knew they were in Oralee."

"I remember Griffin, Catrin, David, and Meghan telling how the Pundles protected them from Krogs during the Crusade, or they would have been killed." Kimball said, rubbing the back of his head with his right hand.

"Sovereign God, as you are a shield to us, please shield our Pundles." Dewey said, bowing his head. "They'll be invisible to all evil, as we were from the Krog." He gave a heavy sigh. "Now, let's take position before Druxin and his evil army get here."

"Desist!" Owen said, hurrying to Dewey. "Griffin opted to have Rowena remain with the warbands, and Kimball conduct the second warband along with you." He paused. "According to Mary, Druxin has thousands of apprentices."

"Second warband follow me." Kimball said, hurrying to mobilize them.

"Tell Griffin, the first warband is right behind you." Dewey said.

"Indubitably!" Owen said, hurrying away.

"Remember, if we need help, I'll send one from the warband to have the rest join the battle." Dewey said, hugging Rowena. "You send them one warband at a time with you leading the last one."

"If things are too overwhelming, I'll have each warband hide behind the shield of the Lord." She gazed into her husband's eyes. "They'll have a difficult time trying to overcome what they can't see."

"Wait a minute!" Dewey said, his eyes gleaming. "I believe, I and Kimball shall go behind the shield of the Sovereign God right now." He motioned to one from the first warband. "Baxter, go tell Griffin the warbands are moving forward behind the shield of the Lord." He gestured with his right hand. "Get right back to us."

"Yes, sir." Baxter said, and quickly ran away.

Arthur and the Squires waited outside the town for Druxin to catch up with his army. "We'll not move until Druxin gives the order." Arthur said, his nostrils enlarged. "Do I make myself clear?"

"We'll not be fooled by the cunning of the Elfdins this time." Elton said, clenching his fists.

Oxford and Winter nodded their heads. "That's for sure. We know who's more powerful in this world."

"Okay." Maddock said, gesturing with both hands. "Let's be quiet before they know we're here." He paused. "Druxin and the Krogs are here."

"Well, my evil army." Druxin said, making a wide grin. "You're looking most formidable." He fingered his black beard. "Arthur, you may proceed with your army of 1,000, followed by Elton, Winter, and Oxford." He gestured towards Maddock. "You'll follow with your army of 5,000." He cupped his hands. "Carbon, Nightshade, Soot, and I will be right behind in case of any trouble." He chortled. "As if a handful of Elfdins are any match against us."

"My only concern is teaching my father where real power is." Arthur said, giving a guttural chortle. "If he hadn't trusted in the Sovereign God, my mother would still be alive." His eyes glared.

"He just sat there and watched her die, while I pleaded with him to do something." He clenched his teeth. "That's a scene an eight-year-old never forgets."

"This is the day for us both to get our revenge on the Sovereign God." Druxin said, his lips curling. "I was the first born and should've been Great Prophet Druxin, but the Sovereign God chose my twin brother, Arthur instead." He fingered his black beard with his right hand. "It's time to get rid of him and his followers."

Mary was the first to see Arthur and his army heading into the town. She had sensed the Sovereign God wanted her to hide in the branches high up in an old oak tree with some stones. As Arthur walked under the tree, she dropped them on his head.

Immediately upon the stones landing on his head, Arthur fell to the ground, and one in his army yelled. "Arthur's dead!"

"Let's move him over on that hill." Elton said, hurrying to Arthur. "Winter! Go quickly and tell Druxin. We'll wait for you to return before proceeding." He paused. "Ask him if I have Arthur's army join mine."

"How can Arthur be dead?" Winter said, grabbing her head with both hands. "Druxin said he's the third most powerful person in the world. "Are you sure he's dead?"

Elton nodded his head. "He's not moving." He gestured with his right hand. "You must hurry to Druxin."

Druxin's face screwed up as he saw Winter running towards him. "What are you doing here?"

"Arthur's dead." She said, falling to the ground.

"What!" Druxin said, his eyes glaring. "How? Who? What?"

"I don't know. We've not confronted any Elfdins. He just fell dead."

"This is the Sovereign God's doing." Druxin said, his nostrils flaring. "Follow me. It's time I led this army to annihilate him and his followers once and for all."

"Elton wondered if you want Arthur's army to join his."

"All armies will follow me and Maddock." He gestured with his right hand. "You run ahead and have all armies wait for me."

"Arthur was like a son to me." Druxin said, as he watched Winter hurry away. "You went too far this time." He said, raising up his right fist. "I'll finish you. You'll no longer be the Sovereign God, but a byword."

"Sovereign God, please don't let them sense me." Mary whispered, hiding motionless as Druxin and his evil army marched under the tree and entered the town. "How am I going to deal with killing Arthur?" She said, climbing down the tree after the army was out of sight. "Sovereign God, I didn't mean to kill him. I thought I would knock him unconscious." She slowly walked over to the hill where Arthur was lying and knelt down.

"Arthur." She said, touching his forehead. "I know you would've killed me, but I didn't mean to kill you." Her eyes filled with tears. "If you hadn't been so set on evil, I believe we could've been good friends." She rubbed his forehead. "I know you know me as Ivey, but my real name is Mary." She sniffled. "I changed my name to Ivey when I joined Druxin because my mother's name was Mary." She bit her bottom lip. "After all, the Sovereign God's mother's name was Mary." She wiped her tears with her right hand. "She died when I was eight, and she loved the Sovereign God. I didn't feel it was right to follow Druxin with her name." She paused. "I didn't know how she could love someone who wouldn't heal her and leave me without a mother." She held her gold cross with her right hand. "After I received my gold cross, everything became clear. I know my mother was ready to be with the Sovereign God." She smiled. "The Bible makes clear he loves us, and he is not capable of doing anything evil." She took his right hand into her hands. "I'm so sorry for killing you."

Arthur gazed up into her eyes. "Mary!"

"Please don't kill me." Mary said, falling backwards.

"I'm not going to kill anyone." He said, tears strolling down his face. "My mother's name was Mary, and she loved the Sovereign God." He sat up. "I, too, was only eight when she died." He touched her right arm with his left hand. "I was so full of anger and hate at the Sovereign God and my father for not keeping her alive that I became another person."

"So did I." Mary said, gazing into his eyes. "However, when Druxin said we were to kill everyone, I knew I couldn't do that."

Arthur stood up, his face covered with both hands, and cried. "While you were touching my forehead, I thought it was my mother. I remembered her telling me this life can be full of storms that are meant to strengthen our faith." He looked up. "She said none of us will ever experience such agony as the Sovereign God did when he died on the cross for us."

"*For I reckon that the sufferings of this present time are not worthy to be compared with the glory which shall be revealed in us,* is what my mother said to me before she died." Mary stood up. "I know she meant her suffering from the disease that was killing her." Her blue eyes filled with tears. "She was through suffering, and I was so selfish. All I cared about was me and that I didn't want her to go."

Arthur grabbed her right hand in his. "My mother said those same words to me. I didn't know what she meant." He wiped tears with his right hand. "She was trying to tell me her suffering was about to be over." He paused. "My father tried to tell me that." He grabbed his head with both hands. "What I put my father through when he was trying to deal with losing his wife." He hung his head. "I was so evil."

"Do you want to ask the Sovereign God's forgiveness?" Mary said, gazing into Arthur's eyes.

"I've been so evil." He hung his head. "I joined Druxin's knights of vile power."

"Nothing we've done matters when we ask forgiveness." Mary said, smiling. "I know, he has forgiven me. He promises *if we confess our sins, he is faithful and just to forgive us our sins and to cleanse us from all unrighteousness.*"

"Sovereign God!" Arthur said, falling to his knees. "I'm so sorry. Please forgive me, and help me to make up for all the evil I've done to my father and others."

Mary took off the other gold cross, and placed it on Arthur who immediately fell backwards. "What was that?" Arthur said, his eyes bulging.

"That's the supernatural power of the Sovereign God who has forgiven you." Mary said, taking his hand to help him up. "This gold cross gives us the supernatural power of the Elfdins in our world." She said, holding her cross close to her chest.

"I need to find my father and make sure nothing happens to him." Arthur said, tears streaming from his emerald eyes.

"Druxin, Maddock and their evil army just entered the town." She said, biting her bottom lip. "We'll have to go around to the backside of the town where the Elfdin warbands are set up." She paused. "Make sure your gold cross is hanging outside for them to see. I don't know if they know who you are."

"I want them all dead." Druxin said, throwing balls of fire. "Find Arthur's father. I'll revenge his death and do what he intended for the Vicar."

"The town seems to be empty." Maddock said, gesturing with both hands. "I don't see anyone."

"I'd advise you all to surrender, or we'll be forced to destroy you." Griffin said. "We'll show our power, while giving you an opportunity to submit." He paused. "There's no reason for anyone to die. Please consider what I've said."

Druxin shot bolts of lightning at the place of the voice. "That's the only surrender you'll get from us."

Immediately, two-edged swords were coming at Druxin and his evil army from all directions. "Druxin!" Elton said. "How do we fight an invisible army? I don't see anyone."

"This is more than I'm aware of." Maddock said, his gray eyes squinting. "I've never encountered power like this. I can't see anyone."

"Remember what I told you. We're invincible." Druxin said, snickering. "It's just part of their trickery to cause fear." His eyes glared. "Send bolts of lightning and balls of fire as quickly as you can in all directions until we've conquered them."

"Grandmaster Druxin!" Maddock and the evil army shouted while shooting bolts of lightning and balls of fire in all directions.

"Something's wrong." Winter said, her voice trembling. "Our bolts of lightning and balls of fire are hitting something and are powerless."

"That's part of the trickery." Druxin said, nostrils flaring. "I used the same trickery on them in Oralee and convinced them they were powerless for 400 years." He shot double balls of fire. "Just do as I say until we defeat them."

Mary and Arthur came in behind the Elfdins with a white flag waving from a stick. "Mary, what are you doing with a white flag?" Rowena said, her eyebrows scrunching together.

"This is Arthur, and we didn't know if any of you knew him." Mary placed her hand on Arthur's right arm. "He had an encounter with the Sovereign God." She pointed to his gold cross. "This is no longer the Arthur who was with Maddock and Druxin." She let out a heavy sigh. "He's concerned about his father who he's treated badly for many years."

"I don't know who his father is." Rowena said, shrugging her shoulders. "All the townspeople are hidden in some cavern under those ruins." She pointed towards the castle ruins.

"No! They're not all there." Chester said, gesturing to his right. "Vicar Downes and I couldn't stay there any longer." He fingered his gold cross. "We figured if the Sovereign God gave us these gold crosses enabling us to have supernatural power, what were we doing hiding underground."

"Father!" Arthur said, running to hug him. "I'm so sorry for what I put you through." He took Mary's right hand. "Mary helped me see truth, and the Sovereign God has forgiven me."

The Vicar looked at Arthur's gold cross and his eyes filled with tears. "Thank the Sovereign God for answered prayer." He hugged his son. "Now, we have to see if we can help Master Godric and the Elfdins overcome Druxin's evil army."

"Wait a minute!" Rowena said, standing in front of them. "You don't understand, they're all hiding behind the shield of the Lord. When behind the shield, we're hidden. It's like we're invisible." Her eyebrows scrunched together. "So are we. It must be the gold crosses that enabled you to see us."

Meantime, the Elfdins became aware that Druxin and his evil army had no intention of surrendering. "Okay!" Catrin said, her voice raising. "Warriors of the Sovereign God wield your power. They're not going to surrender."

"Don't let up until they surrender." Griffin said.

"Splendid deduction!" Owen said, firing two-edged swords and taking down several of the apprentices.

"Indubitably!" Rhonda said, following Owen's two-edged swords with her own and eliminating several more.

"Superlative, my son." Dylan said, downing more apprentices.

"Winifred, Falconer, Fletcher, Gwent, Kevyn, Gwendolyn, Herald." Patrick said. "Let's take out the Krogs."

Their two-edged swords killed Carbon and Nightshade. "No!" Druxin said, keeping Soot behind him."

"Catrin, Drew, Meredith!" Griffin said. "Let's all of us concentrate on Maddock and the rest of you just keep on firing." He paused. "They have no power to withstand the supernatural power from the Sovereign God."

They no sooner let out a continuous stream of two-edged swords when Maddock fell. "Maddock's dead!" Winter said, her eyes bulging. "Plus, they've killed two of the Krogs. We're no match for them." Her voice rose. "We must retreat."

"There'll be no retreating of this army." Druxin said, his nostrils flaring. "We must use defensive methods to stop their two-edged swords."

"You didn't teach us that." Oxford said, his voice shaking. "They're dropping dead all around me." He fell on his knees. "You said there was nothing more powerful than you." His voice rose. "Why aren't you stopping them?"

"Shut up!" Druxin said, sending a bolt paralyzing Oxford. "The next one who says anything negative will be killed." His eyes glared. "Do I make myself clear?"

Chapter 11

David and Goliath

MARY, ARTHUR, VICAR DOWNES, and Chester joined Master Godric, Mistress Edith, Andrew, Deborah, and Matthew. "Master Godric, this is Arthur who's no longer with Druxin." Mary said, gesturing towards Arthur.

"I'm Arthur's father." Vicar Downes said, patting his son on the back. "We've come to see if we can be of help."

"I'm going to fight by my son." Chester said, hugging Matthew.

"I think the Elfdins have things under control." Godric said, rubbing his chin with his right hand. "Maddock is dead, two of the Krogs are dead, and it appears about 4,000 apprentices are dead also."

"Druxin refuses to surrender." Edith said, throwing up her arms. "I believe many more of them will be dead if Druxin isn't stopped."

"I believe that's my responsibility." Arthur said, brushing back his black hair with his right hand.

"No!" Vicar Downes said, grabbing his son's right arm. "Your no match for him."

"All I know is I keep hearing, *thou comest to me with a sword, and with a spear, and with a shield: but I come to thee in the name of the LORD of hosts.*" Arthur said, sighing heavily. "I sense as Goliath was no match for David who fought the giant in the full armor of the Sovereign God." He held his gold cross with his right hand. "Evil is no match for the power of the cross of the Sovereign God."

He tightened his fists. "I go up against Druxin in the supernatural power of the Sovereign God like David."

"I believe I'll be by your side." Mary said, touching Arthur's right arm with her left hand. "Remember the word says, *two are better than one; because they have a good reward for their labour.*"

"*And if one prevail against him, two shall withstand him; and a threefold cord is not quickly broken.*" Vicar Downes said, placing his right hand on Arthur's right shoulder.

"*A thousand shall fall at thy side, and ten thousand at thy right hand; but it shall not come nigh thee.*" Godric said, rubbing his chin with his right hand. "We are to guard you while you concentrate upon Druxin."

"*Thou shalt not be afraid for the terror by night; nor for the arrow that flieth by day.*" Mistress Edith said, placing her hands on her hips. "I believe the Sovereign God is telling us to move in his supernatural power and fear nothing."

"All I know is I'm being urged to face Druxin." Arthur said, clenching his fists and giving a strong nod.

It's no good." Winter said, her voice faltering. "We're getting nowhere. They're dying all around me."

"It's all trickery." Druxin said, his eyes glaring. "I told you I'm the most powerful being in this world. You just stay firm, and we'll defeat them."

Winter nodded her head and slowly slipped backwards to the woods behind the army. "I'm not so sure of his power." She said, crouching behind a large oak tree. "Why didn't I listen to my grandmother who said all evil power is secondhand power from Satan who's a created being? Original power is from the Sovereign God who is the Creator of all powers."

"That's what my mother told me." A voice whispered from the tall grass near the tree.

"Who are you?" Winter said, her voice shaking.

"It's Peter." He said, crawling to her. "Once I saw Maddock die, I ran back here and hid." He sat next to her. "I really don't know why I joined them." He grabbed his head with both hands. "How are we going to get out of this?"

"I believe we'll just stay hidden until it's safe to leave and go back where we came from." She bit her bottom lip. "I think we'd better ask the Sovereign God to forgive us."

"I believe you're right." Peter said, letting out a heavy sigh. "My mother says he'll forgive any sin, if we turn away from it."

They both bowed their heads, and Winter led the prayer. "Sovereign God, my grandmother taught me our free-will gives us the ability to choose what we do. Peter and I chose to do evil with Maddock, and now we choose to do good with you." Her eyes filled with tears. "The Bible says, *but if the wicked will turn from all his sins that he hath committed, all his transgressions that he hath committed, they shall not be mentioned unto him.* Please forgive us and direct us in your will for us. In your Name, we ask. Amen!"

"Amen!" Peter said, smiling. "My mother's probably been in turmoil at my leaving the way I did." He hung his head. "We had a row, and I left. As I was walking, I met Maddock, and the rest is history."

"Hush!" Winter said. "I think I just heard Arthur yell Druxin's name."

"Arthur's not dead?" Peter said, as they both peaked around the tree and saw Arthur and others standing in front of the invisible army.

"Druxin!" Arthur said, standing with Mary on his right with Godric, Andrew, and Deborah. On his left was his father with Edith, Chester, and Matthew.

Druxin's evil army stood still and watched Druxin. "Arthur! What are you doing with them? You were dead." Druxin said, his eyes glaring.

"I once was blind, but now I see." He gestured towards Mary. "She helped me see truth."

Druxin shot double balls of fire at Arthur. "Here's the real truth. It's time for you to die."

"Not so fast." Arthur said, stopping both balls of fire with a swoop of his right hand. "I am no longer an evil apprentice. I am a warrior of the Sovereign God and you have no power over me." He stood tall. "I'm standing in the power of his cross clothed in his full armor." He sent a two-edged sword that hit Druxin in his right shoulder. "Your evil reign is over as of today."

"Soot! Take Arthur down." Druxin said, staggering backwards.

Soot stood still. "What are you doing?" Druxin said. "Take Arthur down."

"Soot!" Arthur said, gazing into her eyes. "You're a good girl." He paused. "I'll protect you."

Immediately, Soot ran to Arthur. When she jumped into his arms, she became the size of house cat. "You stay behind us." He said, putting her down.

"I'm the most powerful being in this world." Druxin said, his eyes glaring. "I'll kill you and Soot."

"Do you repent of your evil?" Arthur said. "If so, you'll not die. If not, I will be forced to kill you as David killed Goliath."

Druxin threw double bolts of lightning at Arthur that fell to the ground. "Here's my repentance."

"As Goliath, you will die." Arthur said, throwing another two-edged sword that pierced Druxin's heart.

As he fell to the ground, the rest of his evil army began to run away. "Not so fast!" Godric said, placing an invisible wall around them. "You all have an opportunity to repent."

Four hundred fell to the ground on their faces, while the rest hurled lightning bolts towards Arthur, Mary, Godric, Edith, and the others. "You've given us no alternative but to destroy you." Edith said, blocking their bolts.

Immediately, Griffin, Catrin, Rhonda, Owen and the rest of the Elfdins came forward and joined Godric, Edith, Vicar Downes, Chester, Arthur, Mary, Matthew and shot two-edged swords killing those who chose to remain unrepentant.

"Get up!" Arthur said, walking over to those on their faces. "If you're serious, you must ask the Sovereign God's forgiveness."

"Sovereign God, forgive me." They all said in unison.

At that, Old came through the crowd holding hundreds of gold crosses. "Put these on." He said, handing out the crosses. "If you're truly repentant, we'll know."

"Wait a minute!" Winter said, as she and Peter ran towards Arthur. "We've repented and were hiding until the battle was over." She hung her head. "We were going to sneak away and go back home."

Old handed them both a cross. "This will confirm your repentance."

Winter put hers on and fell backwards. "What happened?" She said, breathing heavily.

Peter put his on and had the same results. "I don't understand what's happening."

"It's called the supernatural power of the Sovereign God accepting your repentance." Catrin said, punching the air with her right fist.

Rhonda knelt down near Oxford. "This one is breathing, but he's like Matthew and Mary were."

"Let's put a cross on his neck." Herald said, taking a cross from Old. "I heard him disputing Druxin's power." He put a cross around Oxford's neck. "If he was repenting of following Druxin, this will tell."

Oxford just lay still.

"It looks like he wants nothing to do with the Sovereign God." Kevyn said, shaking his head.

"We can't just let him die, can we?" Winifred said, biting her bottom lip.

"Before we heal him, we'll have to imprison him." Griffin said, scratching the back of his head with his right hand. "If not, he'll just try to kill us."

"Then we'll have to kill him." Meghan said.

"Wait a minute!" David said, gesturing towards Oxford. "His eyes are bulging."

"He's sitting up." Fletcher said.

"Please don't kill me." Oxford said. "While all of you were talking, I heard my father's voice say he's forgiven me." He grabbed his head with both hands. "I stole his prized bull, sold it, and joined the carnival." He cried into his hands. "When I met Maddock, I joined his apprentices rather than repenting of what I did to my father."

"It appears, he's repented." Old said, clasping his hands together.

"Okay!" Catrin said, her eyebrows scrunching together. "Time for reckoning with the rest of these."

One by one, the repentant army, received the supernatural power of the Sovereign God. "You're all truly repentant." Godric said, clutching his hands together. "I believe I'm to give an invitation to all who want to be part of our prophet's school."

Out of the 400, only 100 decided to join Godric's prophet school. The rest, along with Oxford felt they had to go home and help their parents on the farms. "I'm sure they could use your help." Godric said. *"For as the body is one, and hath many members, and all the members of that one body, being many, are one body.* In the body of the Sovereign God all have a vital part."

"I believe I'd be more helpful in the prophet's school." Winter said, her voice quivering. "My life has been wasted on evil. It's time to do the work of the Sovereign God. I believe the prophet's school is where I can best serve him."

Matthew hugged his father. "I'm so glad this is over." He paused. "I don't understand how Arthur was able to take out Druxin." He gestured with both hands. "I'm really flabbergasted at how different he is. That's how he used to be before his mother died."

"Apparently, the Sovereign God had Mary knock him out, sent her to talk to him, and he was able to reach into his heart." Rowena said. "The grief of his mother's death made him angry at the Sovereign God and his father for not healing her."

"Once Arthur had the gold cross, he possessed supernatural power." Griffin said, scratching the back of his head with his right hand. "The Sovereign God told him he was like David who slew Goliath."

"It would appear the Sovereign God has chosen Arthur to be the most powerful of the prophets." Godric said, clutching his hands together. "That includes me and Edith."

"We're getting up in age and have no heirs." Edith said, her eyebrows scrunching together. "The Sovereign God has chosen them for us." She gestured towards Arthur and Mary. "It's obviously the two of them."

"I'm so thankful for the Sovereign God allowing me to have this gold cross." Winter said, holding the cross in her right hand. "My grandmother taught me that if we yield to the power of the cross of the Sovereign God, we have power over self to do what is right according to the Sovereign God's will. His resurrection gives us the power to rise above all the power of the devil."

"I wish I'd listened more to my mother." Arthur said, walking towards them with Mary and his father. "She told me the Egyptian magicians looked like they were as powerful as Moses, but God revealed who had the true power when Moses' rod swallowed up theirs." His eyes filled with tears. "When we yield to the power of the cross of the Sovereign God, we have authority or *power over all the power of the enemy.*"

"Amen!" Meredith said, looking into Arthur's eyes. "It took we Elfdins 400 years of a dark age to remember that."

"What I don't understand is what happened to Soot?" Patrick said, rubbing his temple with his right hand. "How did she become so small?"

Griffin scratched the back of his head with his right hand. "I believe when she turned to do good, the evil spell was broken."

"Correct." Godric said. "She reverted to what the Sovereign God had created her to be."

"Why are the Pundles still huge?" Kevyn said, his eyebrows scrunching together.

"It has to be because there's no evil spell on them." Catrin said, twirling her raven black hair around her right forefinger.

"Exactly!" Edith said, placing her hands on her hips. "They were made huge to protect you Elfdins from the Krogs during your Dark Age. The Sovereign God used them to keep a multitude of Krogs from entering the Ravine surrounding Gold Mountain." She paused. "I sense they'll become their normal size when they return to Oralee."

"Prodigious!" Owen said, kicking the ground with his left foot. "The Sovereign God is phenomenal."

"Astonishing!" Rhonda said, doing a two-step.

"He truly is awesome." Godric said.

"He's the only true and living God." Arthur said, his emerald eyes beaming. "I'm so grateful for his mercy to me."

"Me too!" Mary said, hugging her gold cross to her heart.

Epilogue

Two Worlds As One

WITH THE END OF Druxin's evil reign, the Elfdins returned to Oralee. Two separate worlds were as one to the followers of the Sovereign God. Certain Humans were permitted to live permanently in Oralee, while both Humans and Elfdins could visit each world often.

Arthur and Mary were married in the Gold Temple with Vicar Downes officiating. "I've never been so overwhelmed in my whole life." Arthur said, gazing up at the Gold Temple that expressed High Gothic architectural principles. The skeletal structure of columns and arches soared to a hundred-foot vault. Framed in the arches were large stained-glass windows of golden yellow, brilliant ruby red, and sapphire blue. At the altar area were smaller windows of only golden yellow below the multi-colored ones. Under the gold windows was a beautifully carved archway shaped like a cross. The inside of the cross archway was lined with gold. *"Give unto the Lord the glory due unto his name; worship the Lord in the beauty of holiness."* He said, choking up. "This is magnificent. I couldn't have dreamed of marrying in such a place where the Sovereign God's presence permeates everything."

"For with God nothing shall be impossible." Vicar Downes said, his voice quaking. "Here's my son serving the Sovereign God and marrying in the Gold Temple."

"I'm so humbled." Mary said, tears rolling down her cheeks. "Arthur and I are not only honored to be married here, but Master

Godric and Mistress Edith have given us their positions at the Prophet's School." She paused. *"Delight thyself also in the LORD; and he shall give thee the desires of thine heart."*

"We were led by the Sovereign God to have you both take over the Prophet's School with Andrew and Deborah as your assistants." Edith said, throwing up her arms. *"The blessing of the LORD, it maketh rich, and he addeth no sorrow with it."* She paused. "We're greatly blessed to spend our golden years living in our castle here in Oralee."

"Amen!" Godric said, smiling. *"The LORD will give strength unto his people; the LORD will bless his people with peace."* He clutched his hands together. "I love our world, but Oralee is a supernatural world that gives such tranquility." He let out a heavy sigh. "I've never experienced such peace." He grabbed his head with both hands. "I'm overwhelmed to receive such a blessing from the Sovereign God."

"Lordy me!" Old said, clasping his hands together. "I'm so thrilled to spend the rest of my life here." He threw back his head and let out a peal of laughter. "It's especially wonderful to have Saber here with Pearl and Pemberton who now have me full time." He shook his head. "I truly love Pearl and Pemberton being their normal size. There's no reason for Pundles to be large anymore." He paused. *"Give, and it shall be given unto you; good measure, pressed down, and shaken together, and running over."* His lips vibrated as he blew out air. "I've given all possessions owned in my world to Sir Richard and Lady Dawn. However, none are worth more than my being here in Oralee with my Pundles." He said, patting Pearl and Pemberton on their heads.

"I'm so pleased to have horses in our world to ride." Gwent said, laughing. "It sure makes travelling around quite enjoyable."

"Amen to that!" Master Drew said, rubbing his chin with his right hand. "Plus, I truly enjoying riding in carriages pulled by the horses."

"Archer and I are going to live at the Prophet School in the Human World teaching Michael and the other prophets how to be proficient in herbal medicine. Although we possess the supernatural power of the Sovereign God, he also wants us to know how to heal our body's naturally." Vanora said, giggling. "Who would have thought our crusade into the Human World would result in our being instructors." She rubbed her arms with both hands. "*And let the beauty of the Lord our God be upon us: and establish thou the work of our hands upon us; yea, the work of our hands establish thou it.*" She paused. "He has blessed the work of our hands to be able to teach others the proficiency of herbal medicine."

"All I know." Griffin said, rubbing his hands together. "I'm grateful to the Sovereign God for revealing to us that *with God nothing shall be impossible.*"

"Amen!" Catrin said, punching the air with her right fist. "*If thou canst believe, all things are possible to him that believeth.*"

"Great Jehoshaphat!" Owen said, shooting his left fist up in the air. "*For the Lord most high is terrible; he is a great King over all the earth.*"

"*O clap your hands, all ye people; shout unto God with the voice of triumph.*" Rhonda said, doing a two-step.

"*For thou hast girded me with strength unto the battle; thou hast subdued under me those that rose up against me.*" Matthew said, holding the gold cross around his neck.

"Amen!" Chester said, hugging his son. "God is faithful. He answered my prayers by bringing you back home."

"*Great is the Lord, and greatly to be praised.*" Meredith said, gesturing with both hands. "We're here to give glory to the Sovereign God." She looked directly into Catrin's eyes. "You lead us in our worship."

Catrin raised both arms, began to sing, with the others singing along. "*Sovereign God, we worship you. Sovereign God, we worship you. We worship you, our God. We worship you, our God!*"